"Laura is not only an outstanding author but also an inspirational friend who I look up to in so many ways. Her book inspires me to live a pure and fruitful life, the way God has planned. *Hot* made me laugh, it made me cry, and it made me feel blessed to have God's grace glisten between relationships seen and unseen."

—DANIELLE DARAH, communications and entrepreneurship undergraduate student, Miami University

"Laura L. Smith has thoughtfully crafted the true temptations of teens into a tender story of forgiveness and mercy. Her accurate interpretation of the constant struggle to balance living God's Word while living in this world makes her characters believable and relatable. This much-needed book handles its tough topic both delicately and profoundly."

—T. L. BUNDY, English teacher and author

"In *Hot*, Laura Smith coolly addresses the issue of that three-letter word in a way that's current, applicable, and authentic. Every teenage girl must read this book (or she'll look back and wish she had)."

—AMY PARKER, author of *A Night Night Prayer, God's Promises for Boys,* and *God's Promises for Girls*

"It was all of the feelings I have ever felt with trying to remain pure. Thank you, Laura, for tackling a difficult topic that all young girls deal with. This book shows us the importance of God's plan for our purity and provides hope for our own personal lives."

—REBECCA HART, graduate student, Miami University

"I read the whole book in one sitting! I've worked with so many teen girls who would be able to identify with Lindsey's dreams and feelings. Lindsey is not perfect, but she learns from her choices. I've seen in ministry how important it is for young people to get their hearts clean with God and their friends."

—MONIKA ALLEN, missionary, Youth With A Mission

"I started to read *Hot* thinking it would be a book I could pick up in between my homework and busy life. But once I began reading, I found that I couldn't put the book down. It kept me turning page after page in anxious anticipation for how it would all turn out. This book brings hard, controversial issues to the surface and deals with them in a very real way. I loved *Hot*!"

—KELCI HOUSE, student, Miami University

DOWNLOAD
A FREE DISCUSSION GUIDE AT
www.NavPress.com

HOT

A NOVEL

LAURA L. SMITH   AUTHOR OF SKINNY

NAVPRESS

THINK

NAVPRESS®

NavPress is the publishing ministry of The Navigators, an international Christian organization and leader in personal spiritual development. NavPress is committed to helping people grow spiritually and enjoy lives of meaning and hope through personal and group resources that are biblically rooted, culturally relevant, and highly practical.

For a free catalog go to www.NavPress.com
or call 1.800.366.7788 in the United States or 1.800.839.4769 in Canada.

© 2010 by Laura L. Smith

All rights reserved. No part of this publication may be reproduced in any form without written permission from NavPress, P.O. Box 35001, Colorado Springs, CO 80935. www.navpress.com

NAVPRESS and the NAVPRESS logo are registered trademarks of NavPress. Absence of ® in connection with marks of NavPress or other parties does not indicate an absence of registration of those marks.

ISBN-13: 978-1-60006-622-1

Cover design by Disciple Design
Cover image by Veer
Author photo by Kelci House

This novel is a work of fiction. Names, characters, places, and incidents are either the product of the author's imagination or are used fictitiously. Any resemblance to actual events, locales, organizations, or persons, living or dead, is entirely coincidental and beyond the intent of either the author or publisher.

Scripture quotations in this publication are taken from the New King James Version (NKJV). Copyright © 1982 by Thomas Nelson, Inc. Used by permission. All rights reserved; and the *Holy Bible*, New Living Translation (NLT), copyright © 1996, 2004. Used by permission of Tyndale House Publishers, Inc., Wheaton, Illinois 60189. All rights reserved.

Library of Congress Cataloging-in-Publication Data

Smith, Laura L., 1969-
   Hot : a novel / Laura L. Smith.
       p. cm.
   Summary: High-schooler Lindsey has always attracted boys who seem only interested in her body, but when she begins dating handsome senior Noah, she finds the real connection she has craved, but her Christian faith and commitment to celibacy are tested.
   ISBN 978-1-60006-622-1
   [1. Dating (Social customs)--Fiction. 2. Sexual abstinence--Fiction. 3. High schools--Fiction. 4. Schools--Fiction. 5. Christian life--Fiction.]
   I. Title.
   PZ7.S6539Hot 2010
   [Fic]--dc22
                                              2009050470

Printed in the United States of America

1 2 3 4 5 6 7 8 / 14 13 12 11 10

To Brett: thank you for your outpouring of the kind of love described in 1 Corinthians 13 and rarely exhibited in real life. I will never be able to express my gratitude and love to you for being blind to my past. You are integral in every particle of my present and our moments together are what I most look forward to in my future.

ACKNOWLEDGMENTS

God, thank You for the gift of forgiveness. Thank You also for rays of inspiration that nurture the plots and characters You plant in my mind. Without Your love my words are but a resounding gong or a clanging cymbal.

Maddie, Max, Mallory, and Maguire: Thank you for your priceless love. You'll never know how much you warm my heart. I praise God each day for giving me such amazing children. I pray you will always turn to Him to make wise decisions and that you will always be confident in His love and my love for you.

Mom: Thank you for sparking my love for books, both reading and writing them, and for being my number one fan.

Rebekah Guzman: Thank you for believing in me, Lindsey, and her friends. Thank you for being brave enough to take on such steamy subjects. It is your faith and support that ignited these stories to life.

Amy Parker: Thank you for your incredible gift of wordsmithing. You simmered this story taking it from warm to *Hot*. You are an incredible source of inspiration in both my faith and my writing.

Todd Agnew: Thank you for inspiring me, Lindsey, and countless others with your powerful, heated lyrics.

Father John Ferrone: Thank you for homilies that speak

directly to my heart as if "you knew everything I ever did."

Reverend Jim Zippay: Thank you for challenging me in my faith. Your "Sacred Sexuality" series helped me soothe old burns with the calming aloe of God's grace.

CHAPTER ONE

I changed my look this morning. I straightened my curls into poker-straight, shiny locks. I like it. It's sleek. The only problem is, without my curls my headband is too loose and keeps slipping off my head. I had to fix it in the girls' room between classes. So now I bolt toward English with seconds to spare.

As I scurry toward the door, I run smack into Noah Hornung. He's about twice as tall as me. He's running his fingers through his dark hair that seems to naturally spike up in a messy kind of way. He probably can't even see me from up there.

"Man, I am so sorry, Lindsey," he says in a rich voice that reminds me of the dark brown suede vest I splurged on last week.

"No problem." I crane my neck to look at him. How did he know my name, and has he always been that hot? I mean he's always been here. Noah goes to youth group with us at my best friend Emma's church. But so do a ton of other kids. And he always sits with a bunch of guys I hardly know. He lives in my sprawling subdivision, but on the other end. He's a junior, so even when we were kids and played in the neighborhood, he hung out with kids a year older than me. Noah's dark green eyes, topped by thick, dark eyebrows, lock with mine. I feel my cheeks turning as pink as my headband.

Brrriinnngg!

The class bell, announcing that I am officially late, echoes through the vacant hallways.

"We're late," he laughs.

"Yeah, see ya." I cock my head and smile as I duck into my doorway.

Mrs. Pearson shoots me a dirty look as I try to sneak into my row.

I slide into my seat. My books softly thud on the desk. I lift my head to see Noah in the doorway winking at me before disappearing down the hall. Lights dance in my head, like flashbulbs of the paparazzi. His eyes are so big and my fingers itch to touch that messy hair. I don't know much about him, but I feel all tingly and freezing and burning at the same time, like my hand feels when I've held my hair dryer for too long. *Slow down,* I tell myself. *This is the first time he's ever spoken to you.*

I should relax, anyway. Boys and I put together have always been a "Fashion Don't." I've been asked on plenty of dates, but the boys all seem to want one thing: something physical. Nobody wants to listen to me or talk to me or even watch a movie with me. Sometimes I curse the fact that I'm pretty. I know it doesn't seem to make sense. I can't say that out loud to any of my friends. Who would understand?

I was so gawky when I was younger. I remember wishing I could look like my sister, Kristine, so that boys would notice me. Then, in eighth grade, I had eye surgery and said good-bye to my glasses. The orthodontist removed my braces. Kristine gave me a full makeover before I entered high school so I wouldn't embarrass her by being her "nerdy little sister." Now it seems like overnight, I'm not the geeky girl anymore, but I've evolved into the pretty girl I dreamed of being. It's so ironic. Now that I got my wish and people do think I'm pretty, I'm wishing for something else, that boys would be interested in *me*—what kind of music I listen to and what my thoughts on God are and how I feel about my family—instead of what I look like.

Tommy Bayer invited me to his house to watch a movie with his family. That seemed innocent enough. But it turned out his family wasn't even home. So about ten minutes into *Shrek the Third*, he leaned over and tried to stick his tongue down my throat. When I turned my face away from his, he turned from "Tommy Bayer" into "Tommy Bear" and tried to grab every part of my body he could with his grubby paws.

To prevent that from happening again, when Warren Adler asked me out, I suggested he come to *my* house. Wrong! He came over and kept trying to slide his hand in between my legs under the kitchen table. I squeezed my knees together so tight, my thighs ached by the time his mom came to take him home.

A beautiful boy named Brock invited me to our Christmas dance, the Sugarplum Stomp, last year. Mom bought me this amazing dress with a fitted waist. We had a seamstress take it in to fit perfectly, and it had a skirt that flared out just enough to *swoosh* while I was dancing. I told my friends I ended it with him because he popped his gum. The truth is, Brock tried to slip his hands into that gorgeous gown anywhere he thought they could fit.

Maybe I've just been interested in the wrong boys. The underclass guys seem unsure of themselves. They get all nervous and fidgety when they talk to me. Most of the upperclassmen seem so full of themselves. They act like they're doing me a favor if they speak to me.

Which brings me back to Noah. How did he even know my name? I still can't figure that out.

The fifty-minute class takes an eternity. Each second rigidly ticks on the black and white circular clock affixed above the door. I look out the door, half expecting to see Noah winking. I must be going crazy. Clearly, he's gone to class. I struggle to remain still. I have lots of practice from dance team. We are supposed to be like puppets, completely immobile until we're brought to life by music.

Mrs. Pearson lectures about the symbolism of Shakespeare and his description of Queen Mab. I doodle swirly designs on the borders of my spiral-bound notebook with my favorite aqua blue pen. My swirls are like the dreams described in the Shakespeare passage, hard to follow but seemingly purposeful.

At lunch my right foot nervously taps up and down by my plastic chair as I sit with my plate of French fries and a chocolate shake — about the only two things the cafeteria serves that I trust. I wait for my girlfriends to find their way to our table. The cafeteria smells like the old gum that's stuck under the tables and the mysterious gravy the cafeteria ladies ladle over suspiciously bright yellow mashed potatoes. I sip thick, frothy chocolate to avoid looking like a loser as I sit by myself and wait. One by one my friends plop their trays on the table.

"Hey, Linds," Raven says. Today, her thick, dark hair is coaxed into a sixties flip. With her is Emma, who never lost her baby fat, but has gorgeous fiery hair and the eyes of a cat.

"Ladies." Gracie nods. She is the classic beauty. With straight black hair and flawless skin, she's one of the few girls in school I don't have an urge to make over.

With her is Melissa, my partner from dance team, towering over me. "Hi, guys," she says between crunches of the golden apple she's holding.

Emma and I have known each other forever. Melissa and Gracie have been friends since grade school too. Freshman year,

Raven moved here from Atlanta, and she plays on the JV soccer team with Gracie. That's how we all got connected.

Once they're settled, I try to sound as casual as possible.

"So, do any of you know Noah Hornung?"

"Sure." Raven nods. "He plays hockey with my brother." Her eyes are as dark as the black coffee my dad drinks in the mornings, but somewhere in those inky irises, a glint of mischief lurks. She's on to me.

"Really?" I lean over. And immediately, I lean back in my seat, adjusting my icy blue sweater with pink-striped cuffs.

"Somebody has a crush!" Emma sings, her red curls bouncing over her broad shoulders.

I tilt my head and raise my eyebrows, unable to deny it. "So, what if I do? What do we know about this boy? Is he a total dork?"

"Drew's on the JV team, and varsity helps out a lot. Drew says Noah's really nice and helpful and stuff—not like some of the other macho varsity players," Gracie pipes in. Her narrow eyes smile like they always do when she talks about her boyfriend, Drew. "You should come to the games with me."

"Yeah! Come to the games!" Raven cheers, her bag of Cheetos letting out a whoosh as she opens it. "I always sit with my folks, which is fine, but I'd love y'all to hang out with me. Plus Noah's super cute."

"How'd you meet him?" Melissa asks, munching another bite of apple. She's the quiet one in our group. In the spring of freshman year, she confided in us that she's struggling with an eating disorder. I think she's tentative about piping in sometimes, afraid we're judging her. We're not.

"He's in youth group," adds Emma. "But I've never seen you talk to him."

"Yeah, I thought he was." I dip a fry in ketchup. "I never

had talked to him, until right before English. I know this sounds goofy. We just ran into each other in the hallway today—literally, *BOOM*—and he knew my name, which was completely surprising, and I felt something." I shake my head at myself. "I know it sounds cheesy, but it was like we connected or something." To stop anything more ridiculous from coming out of my mouth, I pop a fry in, licking the tangy ketchup so it doesn't drip on my chin.

I look past my friends and gaze out to the chaos of the lunchroom. A group of guys including Raven's brother, Randy, is huddled around a broad-shouldered blond intently engrossed in his Nintendo DS. It's the varsity hockey players. Noah stands in the back, watching his friend defeat electronic enemies, weaving his fingers through his messy hair. He looks up and sees me looking at him. I feel like grasshoppers are jumping inside my body. I drop my eyes and slurp the life out of my milkshake.

"First comes love, then comes marriage, then comes the baby in the baby carriage," Emma sings dramatically in her gorgeous voice.

I roll my eyes. "Please, God, don't let him hear Emma," I say with mock intent.

Melissa jumps in, "At least those babies have a chance at being tall, Linds."

"You might have to marry him for that reason alone," Raven adds.

CHAPTER TWO

"You absolutely *have* to come to hockey on Tuesday!" Gracie squeals. "The JV and varsity teams are scrimmaging each other!"

We're all crammed around a small square table in the mall food court, sipping lemonades and noshing on Auntie Anne's soft pretzels.

"To a scrimmage?" I raise my perfectly plucked eyebrows. "Who goes to a scrimmage? Think how obvious I'd look sitting in the stands by myself."

"Well, Gracie and I will be there." Raven slurps a piña-colada-flavored smoothie.

"Really?" I ask, licking the sweet cinnamon and sugar topping from my fingers.

"Yeah. The guys usually practice at some awful time, like six in the morning. But they actually got a decent ice time, so they're holding a scrimmage. My folks and I were going to watch Randy, but it would be even more fun if y'all were there." Raven flashes her ultrawhite teeth. The honey shade of lipstick she's been wearing really brings out her cocoa coloring.

"I'll go with you." Emma plunges her almond pretzel into gooey caramel dip. "What time does it start, Gracie?"

"It's at four. I could drive." Gracie was the first of us to turn sixteen. Her driver's license has opened a whole new world to us. Now that she can drive, we're no longer completely dependent on parents for transportation. And she's so responsible, none of our folks mind at all. Emma got her license too, but she's been grounded from driving indefinitely. As great as it is to ride with Gracie, I can't wait until I can drive—to have the kind of independence to go anywhere whenever I want.

"I'll be at rehearsal," I say. My brain gears turn. I'd love to watch Noah play. I remember his green eyes shooting invisible lasers into mine across the cafeteria. My heart burns, and a smile creeps up my lips. He must look hot in all that gear. How will I get from the church gym, where we have dance practice, back to the ice rink in time?

"I'll come too." Melissa grins. "It'll be fun. We could ride our bikes over to the rink after practice. If we cut through the park, it shouldn't take more than ten minutes.

"Right, you don't want to be there exactly when it starts, Linds." Raven winks. "*That* would be too obvious."

"Okay, so it's settled." Gracie's silver bangles clang together as she claps her hands. "I'll pick up Emma and Raven around three forty-five. And you two will meet us after dance team."

"I'll have to check with my mom, but why don't y'all plan to head back to my house afterward for dinner? She loves having you." Raven's shiny black hair swings back and forth as she talks.

"With Randy, I don't think we'll all fit in my car to get back to your house." Gracie taps her fingers on the table.

"Randy's car has a bike rack. He can take me, Lindsey's and Melissa's bikes, and whoever else. You don't want all of Randy's stinky equipment in your car anyway. It would smell forever. That stuff reeks!"

"You guys are the best!" I reach out both arms to encompass

my friends into a circular group hug.

"I'm so excited you're all coming!" Gracie's face lights up. "Wait until you see how cute those boys look in their gear!"

"Maybe you can hook us *all* up with hockey players." Emma raises her fire engine eyebrows exaggeratedly like Groucho Marx. "I can just hang out in the penalty box and cozy up to some of the players until our dancers arrive."

I feel a rush like my entire body is immersed in one of those pedicure whirlpool tubs at the spa, and my heart beats as fast as my masseuse's hands pounding my back.

I'm going to be sitting at Noah's scrimmage with my best friends. We'll probably be the only people there, and it will be way obvious that we're scouting players. I don't want him to know I'm there watching him. What if he doesn't like me? But I do want him to know I'm interested. What if he *does* like me?

"Remember when Peter got a penalty in the last minute last week?" Raven recounts.

"Yeah, and then we had to play with too few players, and the Bulldogs had a power play and scored in the last minute."

"Hey, someone should like Peter!" Raven exclaims.

"But he's such a bad boy." Gracie smiles.

"Hands off, Melissa," Emma chastises. "You already have a boyfriend, and bad boys are soooo my type!"

"Ick!" I scream out loud.

"What?" Emma and Melissa turn in unison to me.

"I was just thinking, if I'm coming from practice, I'll be all sweaty and gross."

"You've never looked anything but gorgeous, Linds." Melissa rolls her eyes.

"You should have seen me in junior high." I raise my eyebrows.

"Oh, you were just a tiny bit fabulous then?" Raven mocks.

"No, truly." I nod. "I had these rainbow glasses before I got contacts, and I was all bony and pointy everywhere." We're all so close. Sometimes I forget my friends haven't known me very long, well, except Emma.

"Puh-leeease!" Emma pops the last bite of pretzel in her mouth. "You forgot the braces!" She turns to the others. "She had those awful, thick metal ones and rubber bands going in all directions."

Gracie snorts.

Melissa squints at me as if she's trying to imagine the ugly Lindsey.

Raven leans over to Emma. "Do you have pictures? I mean we could post them online . . . maybe send them to Noah!"

"Ha! Don't you dare!" I eye Emma. She would do it, to be funny. I hope she knows it would devastate me. I think I'm pretty now, but some days I feel that gawky preteen still inside me. And even though my friends are just teasing, it still hurts a little. "I just might need a few seconds in the girls' room right after practice, Mel. That's all."

"Sure." She laughs.

My mind races through my workout clothes . . . something warm enough to wear at the rink. My gray sweat suit is so comfy, but I need something prettier than that. The outfit assembles itself in my mind: powder blue yoga pants, matching hoodie, white tee, and thick white headband. I need to look drop-dead gorgeous.

CHAPTER THREE

"You make me sick!" Melissa shakes her head. She's wearing a men's XL sweatshirt with her dad's alma mater tattooed across the chest. She doesn't have on a trace of makeup, and although her hair is pulled back, the little pieces around her hairline are starting to frizz from sweat. Melissa is adorable. She has enormous green eyes and creamy skin dotted with sweet freckles. She just doesn't spend enough time primping! A little violet eyeliner on her top lid and a swipe of color on her lips would take her from cute to beautiful. She let me make her over once, but I think she did it just to make me happy.

I must admit my outfit pulled together perfectly. I actually changed into a fresh T-shirt in the bathroom and planned ahead by wearing waterproof mascara—can't have smeary eyes! My raspberry ice lip gloss adds just enough color and shine to my lips, without looking overdone.

"Thanks, Mel." I wink at her and sling my brown and pink polka-dot gym bag over my shoulder. "You want a little lip gloss?" I ask. "This color looks great on everybody!"

"No thanks." Melissa kicks back her kickstand and mounts her bike. "Beau has basketball practice. I don't have anyone to impress but you. And you've already fallen for me—I can tell by the way you cleaned up just for me."

Laughing, I pull my sunglasses from my bag. But my jittery hands cause me to stab myself in the eye with one of the tortoise-shell arms. "Ouch!"

"You okay?"

"Mm-hmm." I nod, sliding my shades into their proper place. "Not really," I admit. "I'm really nervous about this Noah thing, and I don't know why." I climb on my bike and push down on the pedal, wobbling a little, then regaining balance.

"Seriously, Linds. Don't freak out about it. Everything will work out the way it's supposed to." Melissa starts down the asphalt path winding behind her church where we practice due to limited gym availability at school. "You really like this guy, don't you?"

"I don't know. I don't even know him! It's just so weird. I've only spoken to him once. And it was about four words." I shake my head. "And it's not like he's gorgeous or anything."

"He's pretty cute, Lindsey."

"Really?" I ask. "I mean, yeah, I think so, and I feel some weird connection. But he's certainly not on anybody's top-ten list. But ever since that day last week, I haven't been able to focus on anything. It's like I'm always on the lookout in the cafeteria and the hallways for Noah, like I'm hoping to bump into him again, like I'm hoping he's looking for me too. Agh, this sounds so gaga!" I brace myself for Melissa's response; now she knows I've lost it!

"Yes, he really is cute. And just because he's not the most popular guy in school doesn't mean he isn't amazing. I mean, look at all of us. None of us are cheerleaders or in *the* popular group, but I think that's a good thing. Raven and Emma and Gracie and you are all gorgeous and funny and talented. I like to think our heads are on a little better than the average sophomore girl's. My guess is boys like Noah are just like us, but on the boy side, you know?" She flips her brown ponytail and wrinkles her cute, freckly nose. "And don't worry about sounding goofy to me. I get all bouncy inside whenever I'm with Beau. Plus, you've had to listen to enough of my wacko life stories!"

We turn onto the sidewalk leading to the rink.

"So, I'm not a crackpot feeling like this?"

"Well, if you are, I am!" Melissa laughs. "I'm just happy I have someone to swap goofy gaga stories with."

"But Beau is officially your boyfriend. I haven't even had a real conversation with Noah, and there's no way of knowing if he likes me — at all!"

"What boy *wouldn't* like you, Linds? You're positively gorgeous and so tiny and smart. It's just a matter of letting him know you're interested, and he'll be all over you."

A taste of bile floods my mouth. I flash back to my Stomp date and his octopus arms.

"Uuugh! Bad word choice, Mel. I don't want him all over me, but I do want him to ask me out."

"Gone" by Toby Mac chimes from my hot pink phone. I carefully slide it from my bag while keeping the other hand on my handlebars and flip it open.

WHERE R U

"Hang on, it's Emma." I put my feet on the ground so I can text back.

B THERE N 5

I read out loud to Melissa,

CUTE GUYS WITH PADS AND SK8S. GOING 2 TAKE THEM ALL FOR MYSELF IF U DON'T HURRY

Melissa pushes off on her bike again and laughs.

LOL CANT U W8? ON OUR WAY

Click. I shut my phone, slide it back in my bag, and race to catch up with Melissa.

"She's a trip." I shake my head and snort. "That's why I love her: she always makes me laugh."

When we get to the rink, there is absolutely no one in the hallways. Our gym shoes echo on the polished white floors.

"I took skating lessons for like a month here when I was a kid, but that was forever ago." I turn my head. "There are two sheets of ice. I'm guessing they're on the full sheet, but I don't know." I keep walking, but I feel like I've had too many Diet Cokes — all jumpy.

Through the enormous glass windows, I see them skating on the full-sized rink.

"Okay, how do we get down there?" Melissa asks, shoving her gloves in her kangaroo pocket.

I'm searching for Noah, but in their helmets and pads all the players look the same. "Uh, this way."

There are a few more people here than I expected. I guess because of the scrimmage. Still, they're mostly parents, so it's easy to spot Emma, Raven, and Gracie in their colorful puffer vests and jackets. They're sitting directly above the penalty box.

"Shew!" I try to hold my breath, grabbing the seat next to Emma. The whole rink smells like the oldest, moldiest sponge that's been left in a sink for months, past its prime, times a thousand. "It's rank in here!" Our voices have a hollow, tinny sound in the arena.

"I warned y'all about the stench," Raven drawls.

"Yeah, there's nothing stinkier than hockey equipment," Gracie adds. "I won't get near Drew until he gets all that gear off and showers!" She holds her nose with one hand and attempts to wave the smelly air away with her other.

Emma leans into me and points. "Noah's right there — number five."

I follow her finger and see him racing down the ice with the puck cradled in his stick. He slaps it into the goal and looks up. He probably heard Emma shouting his name.

I want to duck under my seat or at least hide behind Melissa, but I'm frozen. Noah's head nods as if he's seen me. He skates over to his fellow players, who punch their hockey gloves against his. I'm guessing my cheeks look like I applied my raspberry ice lip gloss to them!

For the rest of the scrimmage and during dinner at Raven's, I try to focus on my friends. Melissa's a mess because Beau's parents forbid him from dating during basketball season. They don't think he has time for school, basketball, and Melissa. Raven decided not to play softball this spring so she can focus on soccer. Emma's annoyed because she always has to babysit her five younger siblings, and Gracie has stories about what life is like with her grandmother living in their house.

But all I keep seeing is Noah running his fingers through his hair. When he pulled his helmet off at the end of the scrimmage, his face was all pink and flushed from the workout. He had been unexpectedly elegant sliding across the ice, despite all of that big, clunky gear. The players were like elephants flawlessly performing ballet.

I begin to strategize how to run into Noah again.

"Lindsey?"

I snap out of my reverie. I look around the table. I don't even know who called my name.

"Earth to Lindsey." Gracie grins. "Randy's talking to you." She smiles even bigger. "I know that faraway look."

"She's thinking about Noah!" Emma squeals.

"Noah?" Randy asks. "Noah Hornung? I was just trying to get you to pass the rolls, but this is even better." Raven's brother gives me that all-knowing look and raises his eyebrows.

Even Mr. and Mrs. Mack laugh.

"Busted." I blush for the millionth time today. "Don't tell, pleeease?"

CHAPTER FOUR

The next day in the cafeteria, I'm picking pepperonis off my pizza. I love pizza. It's hard for even the school cafeteria to mess it up, but the pepperonis have suspicious pools of grease floating in them.

"You don't want those?" Emma asks.

"No." I grimace.

"I'll take 'em."

I shrug and start moving them one by one with the tips of my thumb and pointer finger onto Emma's tray.

"Hey, Lindsey." The voice is so deep and familiar, but I can't place it. I look up. Towering above me is Noah.

"Hi," I manage to say.

He grabs a chair and turns it around backward. His long legs straddle the back of the chair as he thankfully lowers himself to eye level.

"Hi, Raven," he adds.

"Hey, Noah. You ready for Saturday's game?"

"I hope so. Wexley's a tough team."

"Y'all can do it."

"I'll do my best." He ruffles his hair.

"So, Lindsey." He turns back to me. His long-sleeved, gray T-shirt looks so soft, I want to feel it for myself. He looks me directly in the eyes. I can't remember anyone speaking to me with such focus, ever. "I was wondering if you were going to youth group on Sunday."

I look to Emma and back at Noah. "I don't know for sure. I mean, I don't go to church there or anything. I just usually tag along with Emma. I really like Pastor Ed. I think he's—" I twist my lips looking for the right word. "Real, you know, not over the top or anything."

"Yeah, he's cool." Noah unfolds his body from the chair. "Well, if you go, I'll see you there." He places his enormous hand on my shoulder and kind of uses me to push himself to standing. He turns and winks—that same secretive wink from the day in the hallway—and then lumbers away like a giant through a field.

My entire body goes cold like when I first step out of a hot shower into an air-conditioned bathroom. I'm freezing except my shoulder, which is fiery hot.

My friends are silent for about two minutes, which never happens but it's perfectly fine by me. I am frozen like a mannequin. I don't dare watch where he went.

Eventually, it's Emma who breaks the silence. "I guess Randy didn't keep it to himself?"

"He's never been good at keeping secrets," Raven tries to say seriously, but a snicker sneaks from her lips.

We all burst out laughing—so uncontrollably, the whole cafeteria seems to notice. Warm tears trickle down my cheeks. I try to catch them with my fingertips and wipe them upward from where they came, so my mascara doesn't smear.

When the giggles finally work their way out, I turn to Emma. "So, how about youth group?"

She starts to open her mouth, but instead of words a cackle

swirls out like a puff of smoke from a chimney. And the laughter erupts all over again.

/ / /

I spend days planning my outfit for Sunday night. I pull clothes out of drawers and lay them on my white dresser top, complete with shoes, belts, scarves, jewelry, headbands, everything to get the full effect. If after a few minutes or hours or even a day I still don't absolutely love the ensemble, I carefully put each item back in its proper place and start from scratch.

I finally decide on my darkest pair of designer jeans and a beige cashmere cardigan with a Michael Kors white tee underneath. My sand-colored UGGs and brown paisley scarf set it off. I'll look comfortable, pretty, and soft. I'll also be conservative enough for church group, but not frumpy.

"Are you ready, sweetie?" Mom calls from downstairs as I brush the final stroke of mascara on my lashes.

"Sure, here I come."

"I forget—am I taking you to Emma's house or to her church?"

"Emma's first and then her church." I kiss Mom on the cheek. "We're picking her up and giving her a ride."

"Right." Mom grabs her black purse that I covet and digs for her keys. "I'm so glad Emma's church has a dynamic youth group. I love our church, but we're just not big enough to have that kind of program."

I nod. Mom brings this same topic up about every six weeks. It's like she's apologizing or something. I don't mind. I like our church, and I like Emma's youth group. I don't mind going to both. I think it actually gives me a broader view, listening to the different ways both churches approach the same thing. They always end up with Jesus' love, which is all that matters to me.

"Remember what happened when Mike Alcott's son—isn't his name Mike too?—tried to pull something together?"

I remember. "It was awful." I laugh as Mom and I climb into the Prius. "I think maybe four of us showed up for the meeting. We were all too embarrassed to sing because everyone would hear our voices. No one would talk except for Amelia Sorgaf. And she just talked and talked and talked and Mike—that is his name—finally had to cut her off to say the closing prayer."

"Like I said," Mom laughs, starting the car, "I'm glad Emma's church has somewhere you can go. And, Lindsey . . ." She lays her French-manicured hand on top of mine. "I'm so glad you girls want to go and that you have each other as friends."

"Yeah, Em's great." I start pushing buttons on the radio. Mom always changes it to her oldies station, which grates on me.

"You know things are going to be tough in school. Goodness knows with Kristine . . ." Mom's voice trails off like the red taillights of the car in front of us.

I forget about the music for now and look at Mom's silhouette, gray in the dimly lit car. I can tell she's fighting back tears. Mom's a family counselor, which is ironic, considering the state of things with Kristine these days. I guess the doctor can never operate on her own family, or a prophet is never recognized in their hometown—something like that.

Sometimes I'm furious at Kristine. I am both mesmerized and terrified by my sister. She is the epitome of cool. She has that whole cheerleader thing going for her, and her boyfriend makes the entire female population of our school swoon. Of course, she's sleeping with him. As she told me one time, "Safe sex is better than no sex." Whatever that means.

Kristine claims she stays so thin by smoking, and she drinks. "Just a little now and then," she tells me. "It's not like I get loaded or anything." There isn't a party she isn't invited to or a student at school who doesn't know her name.

I see how popular Kristine is, but I also see the post-party Kristine. The one who makes Mom cry with fear and worry when Kristine comes home in the wee hours of the night. The one who gets escorted home by the police when the party she's at gets busted. On the nights that Dad travels out of town for his sales job, I hear Mom sobbing into her pillow long after Kristine passes out on top of her covers. On the nights Dad is home, I hear my parents' strained voices arguing in the dark about what they should do to end Kristine's "path of self-destruction."

I see the morning-after Kristine. The one with puffy eyes and a green face who is snippy and selfish and not-at-all pretty. She smells like an ashtray and goes out to our back porch to puff a nicstick — as she likes to call them — before she'll even speak to anyone. Mom and Dad have thrown away her cigarettes and grounded her for smoking, but she just buys more and doesn't heed their restrictions. I know they're at their wit's end, but she's legal to smoke, which she reminds them of constantly. Mom said something about "picking your battles" and finally agreed she could smoke on the porch, but not in the house.

Odd as it sounds, part of me wants Kristine's life — for people to know me and be envious of my boyfriend and to invite me to all of their parties. But then I remember that's not what it's all about. Jesus has offered me so much more. He already likes me — no, *loves* me. He made me. I hear that, and I know that, but sometimes it's hard to remember.

I pull out my lip gloss and apply a fresh coat in the rearview mirror. We're almost to Emma's. Mom and I have been silent.

We both know what Mom means.

"Mom, I have my faith. I really think Jesus makes me strong. I've seen what's happened to Kristine, and I don't want to smoke or drink." I squeeze her cold, bony fingers, still lying on top of mine. "You know that, right?"

"I know, sweetie." She returns the squeeze. "I'm so proud of you and your decisions. But, if you ever have any questions about anything, promise me you'll come to me first?"

"Sure, Mom."

"Hi, guys!" Emma bounds into the backseat like a spark from a match. "Thanks for picking me up, Mom Number Two!" She squeezes Mom's shoulder and the serious conversation is over. We giggle and listen to music the short drive to Emma's church.

"My mom's picking up," Emma announces as we unbuckle.

"See ya later, Mom. Thanks." I make sure I look Mom in the eye. I want her to know I'm not like Kristine—that she doesn't have to worry. I take one backward glance at my reflection in the window, smooth out my hair (I've decided I like it straight), and rub my lips together, evenly distributing my lip gloss.

Emma opens the door of the building that looks like a white barn. Inside old couches donated by church members form a giant semicircle on the cold white linoleum floor. Since the couches look pretty full, Emma heads for a stack of giant homemade pillows made from scrap fabric in the corner. She grabs a lime green and turquoise circle pillow and plops it on the floor right in front of the brown shag-carpeted stage. On the stage a few band members warm up their instruments. The drum beat pulses through my veins. There's so much energy here, it's like I could reach out and catch God's power in my hands. There are all these kids from different high schools and the music and Jesus, and it's so amazing to me that everyone comes here to get closer to Him.

I have these, what I call, out of body moments every once in a while. When I'm not thinking actual thoughts, not anything that can be formulated into words, but I feel electric and alive, like all my senses have been turned on to God's presence. I am overwhelmed by His power and love and tears actually fill the corners of my eyes. Nothing else matters—not what song the band's playing or if I know anybody here or even what clothes I'm wearing.

"Hey," says a girl with dark curls who's just dropped a pillow next to Emma. I'm sucked back into reality. I recognize her from school. I think she's a sophomore, like us, and maybe in drama, but I don't know her name.

"Hey, Ashley." Emma cracks her gum.

"Hey." I smile. "The band is gonna jam tonight."

Emma taps me on the shoulder.

"What?"

"He's here."

Now my skin is really tingly. It's like that feeling when your foot falls asleep, except my whole body feels like that. I look around at the door, and there's Noah, pulling a ski hat off, revealing disheveled chunks of dark hair. He's with two other guys I recognize from the hockey rink. His cheeks are pink from the cold. He sees me and gives a lopsided grin. He motions to his friends to follow him, and before I can breathe he and his buddies are on a navy blue and maroon striped pillow directly beside me.

"Hey, Linds." He smiles and nods at Emma.

"This is my best friend, Emma," I say, tilting my head on her shoulder. She smells like the green apple hair serum she swears by.

"Hey," Noah answers, then turns to the guy with the brown hair and freckles and the pale-skinned blond. "Wally and Peter."

"Hi," I say, and elbow Emma to say hi too, but she's become

engrossed in a conversation with Ashley.

Everyone crowds in, and I feel Noah's knee press against mine. He is warm and solid and touching me! I look straight ahead, pretending not to notice. It's not a big deal, I tell myself. It's just because we're all squished. A tall, skinny guy with a small silver stud in his nose and a navy and light blue horizontal-striped, fitted T-shirt takes the microphone.

"We're gonna get started, folks." He looks over his shoulder at the band, and I steal a glance at Noah. He smiles with his teeth all in a neat row and winks.

"Ah one, ah two, ah one, two, three, four . . ."

Noah places his large hand on my knee. I swear my jeans are on fire where his fingers rest.

CHAPTER FIVE

"Okay, so fill me in." Raven sounds out of breath as she catches up to us by the glass elevator at the mall.

"Raven!" We all squeal in unison. Emma, Melissa, Gracie, and I take turns hugging her.

"What do you want to know?" Emma asks coyly, tossing her fiery curls.

"Puh-llleeease!" she says in her rolling voice. She has on a neon orange fuzzy V-neck sweatshirt under her North Face jacket. "Everything I missed while we were traveling the country looking at colleges for Randy!"

"First of all, we missed you." Gracie smiles. "How was the trip?"

"Okay, I guess." Raven shrugs. "Some of those schools are really cool. I think college will be awesome, but all that time in the car was a *d-r-a-g*."

"At least you got out of school for a week." Emma smiles.

"I still had to do all the work, but at least I got back in time for Friday night at the mall." Raven shimmies her shoulders. "That is *good* timing!"

"I absolutely positively have to go into Vicky's," I interrupt as we pass the pink storefront with capital gold letters. On cue, my friends all turn in with me in a giant clump. It's kind of like one of our dance team formations, only without the music and boots.

"What are you getting in here?" Melissa's green eyes remind me of Sam-I-Am's eggs, they're so wide.

"You know, bras, panties. I am so in need of new stuff." I start browsing through the PINK section.

"These are too cute!" Raven squeals holding up a pair of cotton lavender boy shorts with white vertical stripes.

"So cute!" I nod. "You should get them. Looks they have a matching tank bra."

"I didn't even know this stuff existed." Melissa shakes her head. "My mom just buys me white, beige, and black, you know?"

Tall, gorgeous models with angel wings attached to their shoulders flash from TV monitors in every corner. Music pulsates almost too loudly to think.

"Oh come on, Mel." I pick up a black, lacy nightie and toss it at her. "Live a little."

"Ahhh!" she screams and tosses it back to me like a hot potato.

"Kristine has all kinds of stuff." I raise my eyebrows. "I guess I learned from her — and tamed it down a bit — that your underwear can be pretty, too, not just your clothes."

I decide on three cotton bra-and-panty sets in cute pastel patterns. Not that I even need bras. I'm so tiny, I buy the AAs with a little padding. I don't buy anything remotely racy. That stuff makes me nervous, but I do like my underwear to match my outfits. There's something satisfying about having everything coordinate.

"And then there's Lindsey and Noah," Emma says to Raven.

I turn from the counter and smile.

"What happened?" Raven asks.

"Nothing." I roll my eyes and smile. "He was at youth group and sat next to us and put his hand on my knee." I feel all bouncy just thinking about it. I recreate it in my head: the song the band was playing, the warmth of his hand, his soft voice as he leaned over after the final prayer, his lips tickling my ear. All he said was "See ya," but I felt like I was going to explode.

"And?" Raven asks.

"And . . ." I sign my name to Dad's credit card. He gives me carte blanche. I think he feels guilty for traveling all the time, so he lets Mom, Kristine, and me shop whenever we want to make up for his absence. I grab my bag by the handles. "And we've chatted a few times in the halls and the cafeteria this week. Nothing major, but he always smiles like we're in on some big secret together, and it makes me feel all crazy! Stay tuned."

"Where to next?" Melissa asks as we amble out of the store.

"All that underwear made me hungry." Emma announces. "How about the food court?"

"I could go for one of those pretzels." Raven nods.

I'm in the back of our pack, my mind still reliving Sunday night. We head toward the escalators.

"Hello, ladies . . ." It's Noah and his best friend, Peter! I feel like I've swallowed a watermelon. I'm sure my friends have answered in some way, but I've become deaf and mute. He is sooo cute! His eyelashes are really long and dark and frame those round eyes to always give him the expression of a little boy who's just gotten away with something.

"Meet us down there," Gracie calls and ushers Emma and the others down the escalator. Peter, a blond with an army buzz and silver wire-rimmed glasses, follows them, making kissy faces at us as he rides backward.

"Where have we been shopping?" Noah asks, flicking my bag.

My cheeks must be as pink as my bag. "Umm, you know, we're headed to the food court. Do you want to join us?" I dodge the subject of underwear.

"I just want to know what's in the bag." He cranes his tall head to peek inside, which of course is hopeless, because everything is wrapped in tissue paper.

"You're ornery." I slap him on the arm.

"You're hot." He grins and leans down and kisses me for one split second smack on the cheek as if it were the most natural thing in the world to do. He smells like fabric softener and wintergreen gum. I blush all over. His mouth felt so warm and perfect on my skin. This is nothing like when those creepy boys groped me. I'm not grossed out, and I don't want to push him away. I'm actually wondering how I got so lucky for him to kiss me, and how I can make him do it again.

"You might not think so if you really saw what's in the bag," I say. My heart must sound like rapid fire from a machine gun.

"Let me see then." He pries open the bag, and I let him.

What am I doing? I'm letting Noah look through my underwear! It's not like I have it on, and it's not like it's see-through or lacy. I think I want to show him I'm not that kind of girl. Pink polka dots and turquoise stripes always seemed innocent to me before now.

"Cute." He looks me up and down, contemplating.

Oh, please don't let him be wondering what underwear I'm wearing right now, which happens to be white Scottie dogs on hot pink to match my hot pink sweater and denim skirt.

"So, Lindsey..." He hooks his arm in mine like a waiter in a fancy restaurant escorting me to my seat. It feels so natural to be walking arm in arm with him like this. This must be the difference between a guy liking me, like those others, and me actually liking him back—*really* liking him back.

"Yeah?" I strain my neck and look way up into his face.

"When are you and I going to go out on a date?"

A puff of air escapes my lips. *Stay calm*, I tell myself. *Stay calm.*

"I guess you would have to ask me first." I look down at the gray and white marble floor, anxious for his answer.

"Hmmm, that sounds reasonable." His gym shoes are untied, laces clicking on the floor step after step. We hop on the escalator heading toward the food court and our friends. My stomach feels like it's twisted into a pretzel shape. "So, how about it?"

"How about what?" I ask, unable to look at him. I feel a bit faint, like the moving stairs might fall out from under me at any second.

"How about you go out with me?" He leans in a little closer.

"I can't go on car dates," I blurt out, ruining the perfect moment.

"It doesn't have to be in a car," he whispers, thankfully helping me off the silver stairs before I trip.

I am elated. It's like the feeling when I made the dance team, only more intense. Unfortunately, I can't savor the moment. From the left side of the food court Emma frantically waves her arm to get our attention.

"Then, what should it be?" I ask, knowing it doesn't matter what he says. I want to go.

"How about . . ." He takes his arm out of mine and strokes his chin where it looks like there's actually razor stubble. He shaves! "How about I come over to your house tomorrow night, and I'll bring a movie?"

"Really?" I ask, wanting to pinch myself.

"Really." He grins again as we reach the group. He grabs a handful of Peter's french fries.

My insides feel like melting butter, but I can't scream or dance or hug my friends. Not yet. I just sit down in the empty chair between Gracie and Raven and Noah flops in the empty chair next to Peter. Everyone else is already munching on their food, which is fine, because I don't think I could eat a single bite.

Apparently, Noah does not feel the same way. After some chatting and goofing around, he scavenges his way through everyone's leftovers, and then Peter announces they better get to practice.

"Practice on a Friday night?" I ask.

"Gotta skate when there's ice time." Noah shrugs.

"See ya ladies. It was a pleasure running into you." Peter bows, Noah waves, and they're gone — just like that.

"Ahhhh!" I scream, when they're out of earshot.

"How did he know you were going to be here?" Gracie asks.

"I have no idea!" I reach in my purse for lip gloss. It calms me to reapply it.

"I do." Raven raises her left eyebrow. "I had Randy bring me here."

Still seated, I tap my feet on the floor like I'm dancing. "He kissed my cheek!" I lay my hand where his soft lips must have left an imprint. "And he asked me out!"

"Congrats!" Gracie pats me on the back.

"Welcome to the wonderful world of hockey." Raven smiles.

"He asked me out." I shake my head.

CHAPTER SIX

"What'cha lookin' for?" Kristine asks and plops on her bed. I'm standing in her closet, sifting through the tops she haphazardly piles on her shelves and floor.

"I don't know, Krissy." I shake my head. Admitting defeat, I lie down on her bed next to her. "Noah's coming over tonight, and I want to look gorgeous—only you're the gorgeous one, so I thought, maybe . . ." I stare at the ceiling. "Anyway, sorry I was in your closet without asking."

"I don't care, sweetie." She rubs my leg. "Who's Noah?"

"You know Noah Hornung. He's a junior, on the hockey team and lives on the other side of the subdivision, down by the creek."

"And you've got it bad for him!" She laughs that beautiful Julia Roberts laugh of hers.

I know I'm blushing again, but since I'm lying flat, she can't see.

"I'll take your silence as I'm so right about this." Kristine stands up and walks toward her closet. "You're just so flat, Linds, that I'm afraid my tops will sag on you." She sticks out her swimsuit model chest. "You'll definitely want to wear something fitted. And please, wear a padded bra!"

My phone vibrates in my pocket. I flip it open to see who texted me.

FUNNY OR SCARY?

It's from Noah.

I smile, picturing him flipping through DVDs. I type back.

FUNNY

I wait anxiously in case he sends anything back.

C U SOON

I let out a huge sigh.

"That was him, I take it." Kristine bats her eyelashes.

I nod.

"Okay, sis, let's get to work on you."

By the time Kristine is done with me, I look maybe the best I ever have. She flat-ironed my hair poker straight. She does it much better than me because she can reach all those crazy underparts without breaking her neck. I have on a comfy cotton white camisole and Kristine's turquoise velvet blazer over it. Even though I would have bought a smaller size, it will do since I'm wearing it unbuttoned over something. I have on my favorite jeans and these darling black boots with stitching and three-inch heels. The extra height won't hurt with Noah. I soften the whole ensemble with a turquoise and black silk paisley scarf tied around my head like a headband.

I brush my teeth and gargle—fresh breath is a must—and spritz on Burberry perfume. I spin in the mirror for Kristine.

"You're smoldering." She nods, approvingly. "Some of my best work."

I laugh.

"Now I've got to do my actual best work. You're not the only one with a date tonight." She walks into the bathroom and turns on the water.

I retreat to my bedroom and close the door. I sit on my bed in the rare silence of the house. My iPod is turned off, Kristine's in the shower, Dad's not due back from his business trip until late tonight, and Mom's downstairs. I breathe in and breathe out, trying to relax.

Dear Jesus, Thank You for bringing Noah into my life. He makes me feel so good about myself. He is funny and charming, and I'm so thankful he's a Christian. I've been asking You what I should do about boys, and I think he's the answer You've sent me. Help me to be myself around him. Amen.

I feel my shoulders relax after praying. I sit quietly, enjoying the calm.

Ding dong.

I'm so excited to see Noah. I don't even look in the mirror again before walking downstairs. I'm halfway down when I hear his voice.

"Hello, Mrs. Kraus, I'm Noah Hornung. Is Lindsey home?"

My heart feels like the Grinch's, growing several sizes. He is wooing my mother with manners.

"It's nice to meet you, Noah. Lindsey is expecting you. Won't you come in?"

I reach the landing just as he enters.

"Hi." I smile, not knowing exactly what to do.

"Hi." He looks me up and down, but not in a wolf kind of way, more in a he-likes-the-way-I-look way, then taps the DVD case. "I think you're going to like this one."

"You two go on back to the family room. I'll make some popcorn." Mom takes off, leaving us alone.

"You look awesome!" He raises his eyebrows.

"Thanks." I turn around, a little embarrassed but completely flattered. It was just the reaction I was hoping for! I lead him into the family room, where he heads straight to the DVD player.

"So, what did you bring?" I ask.

"*The Mighty Ducks!*" He grins goofily.

"*The Mighty Ducks?*" I look at him blankly.

"Sure, if you're going to be a hockey groupie, you need to see this movie. It is the ultimate feel-good hockey flick." He slides the shiny disc into the player. "You picked funny." He grabs the remote and plops down onto the couch. He pats the spot next to him for me to sit.

"Hockey groupie?" I say, pretending to be offended as I lower myself on the couch. I recognize the clean scent of Tide. His mom must use the same detergent as mine. His thigh touches my thigh. He feels so warm.

He looks away from the screen and into my eyes. Our faces are so close he could kiss me. "Anyone who attends a scrimmage is being sucked into the wonderful world of skates and pucks."

"Or, they're falling for one of the hockey players," I retort, maintaining his gaze. I'm amazed by my bravery, but this flirting game is exhilarating. We're both putting ourselves out there a little. I can't wait to hear his reply.

"Then, maybe you won't be a groupie." The corners of his lips curl in a sly grin. "Maybe you'll be a hockey girlfriend."

"I hope you like lots of butter," says Mom, placing the big blue ceramic popcorn bowl on the coffee table in front of us.

"Yum! Thanks, Mrs. Kraus," Noah says, scooping out a big handful. As the kernels fall into his mouth, he winks at me, somehow sealing our conversation.

"You're welcome." Mom looks at me and raises her eyebrows in approval. "Lindsey, I'll let you get drinks. I didn't know what you two wanted."

"Thanks, Mom."

I stand up. My body temperature drops ten degrees, and I'm able to breathe more easily. "What's your poison?" I ask. "Diet

Coke, water, Gatorade?"

"Gatorade." Noah nods, watching the screen. "Hurry, though. The previews are almost over, and you don't want to miss anything."

I roll my eyes and disappear into the kitchen. *Girlfriend.* He definitely said girlfriend. Does that mean he already thinks I'm his girlfriend or that I just might be able to pass the test and move up to girlfriend status? I can count all of our conversations on one hand, yet it's like he knows exactly how to make me smile and says exactly what I want him to say, and it's all so natural, not rehearsed like some of the guys in Kristine's group.

I take a sip of Diet Coke. The sweet bubbles tickle my tongue.

"Soda?" Kristine laughs as she traipses through the kitchen in a see-through, ruffly blouse, painted-on jeans, and my new patent-leather ankle boots. "How cute. Anyway, I figured the jacket for the boots was a fair trade." She points to her feet. "Okay?"

"Sure." I can't argue, but I haven't even worn my boots yet. They were my last purchase at the mall yesterday. I pour orange Gatorade and listen to it crackle over ice cubes.

I grab our glasses and head into the family room. Kristine stands in front of Noah, with that cheerleader smile on her lips.

"I wish we could cheer for your hockey games," she says and lowers her eyelashes. "I think it's because hockey and basketball overlap, but still, all you boys banging into the glass, it would be, like, so much fun."

"Yeah, it would be great having you all 'rah-rah' for us." He raises his left eyebrow.

My insides freeze, like my blood is a Slushie, barely able to move through my veins.

Kristine leans way over to grab a handful of popcorn. She

lingers for a second longer than necessary—and then another. Even from where I'm standing, I know her shirt gapes, showing off her ample cleavage. I pull my eyes from her to Noah. His eyes are glued to her chest.

My frozen insides do a three-sixty and start to boil. *Why?* She has the most popular boy in school. She said she didn't even know who Noah was. Why would she do this to me?

I force myself to walk forward. "Did I miss anything?"

"Gotta run, kids." Kristine smiles sweetly at me. "There's a party at Wesley's tonight. If you get bored with your movie, come and join us." She looks back at Noah, pouts her lips, and slinks out to the garage, car keys jingling.

"Like we would want to come," I say under my breath.

"Who's Wesley?" Noah asks me.

What if he wants to go? What if he wants to see more of Kristine? What if I've dissolved into my old, ugly self compared to the magic allure of my sister?

"Her boyfriend," I throw out like a line drive. Better to let Noah know he doesn't stand a chance with her anyway.

"Note to Lindsey," he says, pushing the pause button, "please don't ever flirt with other boys that way." Noah shakes his head. "I want everyone to know you're my girlfriend and definitely not available." He slides his arm around my shoulder, and in an instant everything is perfect. He doesn't like Kristine. He likes me. He called me his girlfriend, and that strong, warm arm is protecting me from any harm that could ever come my way.

"Promise," I say, not able to verbalize the eddy of worries and relief and joy contained inside my heart.

"Now," he announces, "the moment we've all been waiting for." He makes a drumroll sound with his tongue and pushes Play.

For the next two hours, we laugh and cheer for the Ducks

and Coach Bombay. We work our way through the whole bowl of popcorn and slurp down our drinks. We pause about two-thirds through to get ice cream. Mom roams in and out of the room, getting a magazine, refilling our drinks. I like that she's around, but not intrusive.

When the movie's over and Mom's said goodnight, we clean up our dishes in the kitchen. Noah puts his elbows on the island and leans forward. His cheeks are rosy and his white Henley shirt sits kind of crooked on his frame.

"So, youth group tomorrow, Linds?"

"I was planning on it, but I need to check with Emma." I nod.

"You seem to get there before me." He stands and rubs his left hand through his hair. "Will you save me a seat?"

"Promise," I smile, thinking he doesn't have to ask. My eyes will be stuck to the doors, counting the seconds until his arrival.

"You've been doing a lot of promising tonight." He takes a step closer to me.

"Is that a bad thing?" I ask, feeling the air between us get smaller and denser.

"It's a great thing."

There is only an inch of air separating our bodies now, and it's as thick as Jell-O.

His head punches through the invisible barrier and brushes his lips against mine. My heart flutters like the eyelashes of a starlet. I close my eyes and breathe in his warm, somehow sweet scent. But then an alarm goes off in my head. I know what's next, and I dread it. He'll try to shove his tongue between my closed lips, slide his hands up my front, fumble for my zipper, as if I'd let him even touch it. That's what they all do. But, none of that happens. He's not like the others. He pulls his lips, sweet from the chocolate sauce on our sundaes, away from mine and straightens himself.

"I've gotta go. I promised my parents I'd be home." He pulls on his coat and takes my hand in his. My hand! As in old-fashioned hand holding! And he walks with me to the door.

"You are officially initiated into the hockey girlfriend club." He mock-knights me with his arm posing as the sword, tapping my shoulders and head.

"Initiation was so easy, anyone could join," I tease.

"Oh, no, my dear, not anyone. Not anyone at all." Noah backs up a step and looks at me. "You're different, Lindsey."

And then, for one more split second, I'm a princess in a fairy tale. His mouth dances across mine, just long enough for me to feel its warmth, to taste its sweetness.

"I—," I start to say, but don't know what to say. I can't say I love him. Saying "I like you" sounds trite.

"You what?" He cocks his head.

"I had a great time tonight," I manage.

"Lucky for you, there's a *Mighty Ducks 2* and *3*." He grins. "See ya." And he opens the heavy front door with a loud squeak. He shoves his hands in the front pockets of his jeans and strolls down the driveway to the curb where he's parked his black Honda Civic. I stand by the door watching him a minute, but he doesn't glance back. Since I don't want to look like a lunatic standing there, I close the door and lean against its solidness.

I run upstairs and fire up my computer. I know it will take him a couple of minutes to get home, so I try to take my time getting ready for bed. I carefully hang Kristine's blazer back in her closet. I rezip my boots once they're off to hold their shape and put them in their place on my shoe rack. I brush *and* floss my teeth.

How long has it been? Three minutes? Four? Not long enough. I wash *and* moisturize my face. I pull on comfy yoga pants and a soft tee to wear as pajamas. I finally allow myself to check the clock. Twelve minutes since Noah left.

My fingers race to Facebook. There's his picture. Wow! He's so cute I could stare at it all day. Okay, his relationship status is "Single." I try to reassure myself he might not even be online. I mean he's barely been home. As I'm talking through all of the possibilities in my head, he shows up as an "Online Friend."

It's freaky knowing that he's on and I'm on and I can see what he's doing, well sort of. I feel like Big Brother.

Blip. I get a message in my e-mail box. "Noah said on Facebook that you two are in a relationship. We need you to confirm that you are, in fact, in a relationship with Noah Hornung."

My heart is like a frog's expanding throat, about to burst.

No-brainer. I click on the message and instinctively confirm. *Click.*

It's done. It's official. Now the whole world can see what my heart feels.

I get an IM.

`u r so much more than a groupE.`

CHAPTER SEVEN

Emma's mom is late. I stand in the hallway near the front door. I flick on the bathroom light and reapply my lip gloss. I unzip my black puffy vest to see which way looks best. Zipped. I look at my watch again.

Beep! Beep!

Even though I've been waiting for them, the sound of the horn startles me, and I drop my lip gloss lid.

The tension in their Jeep is thick. Emma and her mom have clearly been fighting, so I don't mention that we're running late or that I'm supposed to be saving a seat for Noah. In fact, I don't say a word and neither do either of them the whole way to youth group. Getting out of the car is a relief, like someone's taken a gag out of my mouth.

"What happened in there?" I ask as the Jeep zooms away.

"Mom completely forgot she was taking us tonight and acted like I was so selfish because I expected her to take me to church, which by the way she agreed to last week!" Emma shakes her head. "It's church for crying out loud! I didn't ask her to take me to the mall!" Emma yanks open the barn door, and the vibrations of the electric guitar jamming "Jesus Freak" rush at us. "She is such a case," Emma mutters.

I scan the room. Where is he? Then I see the back of Noah's

messed-up hair. He's wearing an untucked red-and-black-checked flannel shirt and faded jeans. He and his friends are singing and elbowing each other and definitely aren't on the lookout for us.

Emma starts weaving her way through the crowd toward some open seats.

"Can we sit by Noah?" I ask, a little embarrassed.

"Whatever," Emma grunts, "if there's even room."

I didn't mean to upset her or seem insensitive to her fight with her mom. We just need to find a seat, and we really can't talk about her fight over the singing, and I'd already promised Noah. Noah and his friends stand in front of the biggest couch. There are four of them. I honestly don't know if there's room on the couch with all their sprawling hockey bodies. It's impossible to tell while they're standing. What if we get over there and there's no place to sit? I'd look like a fool in front of Noah and his friends and make Emma even angrier. I feel all yuck inside like I've spilled grape juice on a gorgeous new white blouse.

When we're an arm's length from the couch, Noah grabs my arm and Emma's arm and pulls us to either side of him. "Hey, ladies," he whispers, "thanks for saving us these great seats." He winks at Emma, who actually smiles back at him. He's truly a miracle worker to pull Emma out of one of her funks.

We sing two more songs. I'm self-conscious next to Noah. One, I have a horrible voice. Emma sounds like she's on MTV, so I just kind of sing quietly and let her voice fill in all my flats and sharps. Two, some people get more into it than others, and I don't know how seriously Noah takes all of this. I mean, he's here every week, but where does he stand with Christ? For that matter, where do *I* stand with Christ?

Pastor Ed takes the microphone from the lead singer. He's

tall and thin with pale skin and wavy, sand-colored hair. He has bushy eyebrows and big, round, green eyes that kind of make him look like a Muppet when he gets going.

"Thanks, guys." He nods to the band. "Thanks for getting the crowd warmed up, because tonight we're going to talk about a really hot topic." He looks around the room for dramatic effect. "Sex."

It is as quiet in this barn as that house in *'Twas the Night Before Christmas*.

"That's right, folks, I said, *sex*!" Ed looks around the room.

I look down. I know I'm blushing. This is too embarrassing! How can I sit next to Noah while a sex talk takes place?

"I feel like a bad comedian who's just told his biggest bomb." Ed laughs. And it's true. The room is silent. Everyone is looking anywhere but the stage. I don't know if the crowd is more uncomfortable for themselves or for Ed having to stand up there and talk about sex.

I become aware of things I haven't noticed before, like the room smells like cleaning supplies and sweat, and there's a slight hum from the amplifier that the guitarist hasn't turned off all the way.

"I told you it was hot."

A few nervous giggles bounce from different corners of the room.

"I'm sure you all know by now about the birds and the bees."

Peter makes a buzzing sound and flies his fingers to land on Noah's shoulder.

"But, do you really know God's plan for you and sex?" Ed takes a sip from his bottled water. "Yes, I said 'God' and 'sex' and 'you' all in the same sentence. You see, God invented sex. So, as dirty and scandalous and embarrassing and forbidden and taboo as we like to think sex is, it is actually a beautiful, amazing gift from God." He walks around the stage.

I sense guys all around the room nudging each other. My eyes are glued to Ed's feet, which happen to be wearing beat-up Converse high-tops.

"This does not mean having sex at will is okay. As with most truly great gifts, sex comes with an instruction manual." Ed looks around the room. His eyes hone in on a white-haired kid with a silver hoop in his nose, wearing a black T-shirt.

"Ryan, what's the best thing you got for Christmas this year?" It's a relief to hear at least one sentence without the word *sex* in it. I lean back a little and allow myself to turn to where poor Ryan has been put on the spot.

"Uh, the newest Guitar Hero for my Wii." Ryan shrugs.

"Did it come with instructions?" Ed asks.

"Sure."

"Emma." Ed wheels around and stares directly at our couch. "How about you?"

Emma looks at me and back to Ed.

"What's the best thing you got for Christmas this year?"

"An iPhone." Emma stands up, slips her phone from her pocket, and holds it up for the crowd. "And, yes, Ed . . ." She flashes a huge smile. "It came with instructions."

"Thank you, Emma."

Emma bows with a flourish before sitting back down. She loves to have the stage.

"And, if you started banging your little brother on the head with your guitar accessory or tried to use your phone without charging it first, would they work? Maybe, maybe not. But, even worse than not working, they could be broken . . . destroyed." Ed nods to the guy in back who works the audiovisual stuff. A Bible verse flashes on the overhead screen.

"In Genesis, we see how excited Adam was when God made Eve for him." Ed reads the verses aloud:

"At last!" the man exclaimed. "This one is bone from my bone, and flesh from my flesh! She will be called 'woman,' because she was taken from 'man.'" This explains why a man leaves his father and mother and is joined to his wife, and the two are united into one. (Genesis 2:23-24, NLT)

The worship band walks back on stage and starts strumming their guitars.

"And now a word from our sponsors, to give you all a break." Ed smiles and sits down.

The lead singer's powerful voice cuts through the room, "Blind man stood by the road, and he cried. . . ." Noah leans back, and our shoulders touch. I smell his minty soapiness and can almost inhale the warmth from his shoulder.

"Steamy stuff, Linds," he whispers in my ear as the band begins to sing.

"Very." I tilt my head into his and feel his rough hair tickle the side of my face.

After the intermission, consisting of the song, popcorn and soda, and a get-to-know-your-neighbor game, Ed calls us back to our seats.

"On a chilly night like tonight, I think I'll go home and build a fire in my fireplace. There are few things more comforting and cozy to me than watching those beautiful flames dance and listening to the musical crackle of a fire while it brings warmth to my home."

I picture Noah and I snuggled up in a quilt by our fireplace. It isn't hard with his body aligned with mine.

"Now the thing about fire is, as amazing as it is in my fireplace, it's one of the most dangerous things known to man if it sneaks out of the fireplace. It burns precious belongings, destroys homes, and even kills."

Ed pulls a match from his pocket and lights it. *Pchheeeuu!* The match ignites. The scent of sulfur seeps into the air. Ed allows it to burn until it almost singes his fingertips. He blows it out. Smoke curls toward the ceiling, and the room is silent.

"Sex is like that. In the hearth of marriage, God has created something beautiful and intimate that can warm your soul and nurture your relationship with your spouse. But, sex outside of marriage is like a fire outside of the fireplace. It can burn you and destroy you. It could be treacherous."[1]

Despite Noah's warm presence beside me and all this talk about heat, a shiver streams down my scalp like cool water in the shampoo sink at the hair salon, then spreads over my entire back and down my arms to my fingertips.

"You okay?" Noah asks. His lips flutter on my ear.

"Yeah, just a chill, that's all." I keep my eyes glued to Pastor Ed. It's hard to think about Noah's soft lips when Pastor Ed is warning against the dangers of sex.

Noah slides his arm around my shoulders in a comforting, concerned way. I lean into his safety. He pulls me closer.

"I'll keep you warm."

I miss most of Ed's closing prayer between snuggling next to Noah and trying to process tonight's lesson.

Outside in the parking lot, Emma elbows me. "So which was

---

1. Fireplace analogies were inspired by Pastor Jim Zippay's sermon on Intimacy, June 2007.

hotter tonight: Ed's message or you and Noah?"

"Stop!" I slap her arm, completely embarrassed. I tilt my head to make sure no one's listening. Almost everyone's gone. There's just a small group of four or five kids hanging out by the doors, laughing. My brain buzzes like birds and bees.

I whisper to Emma, "I just—I guess I never really thought about it from God's side before. I mean, I know I'm not supposed to have sex before I get married, but I never really thought about why."

"Do you buy into everything Ed said?" she asks.

"Yeah, I think so. I mean there's stuff like AIDS and pregnancy, which are plenty scary, but the idea of that fire gave me the shivers. I don't want to get burned."

"What if other things in life have already burned you?" Emma asks. Her breath looks like the smoke from Kristine's cigarettes as it hits the brisk night air.

I know her parents argue a lot, and it's driving her crazy. I know she gets annoyed when she has to babysit all her little brothers and sisters. She usually won't talk about it, though, but she said 'burned,' and that's a strong word. "Is it that bad, Em?" I squeeze her hand.

"Nah." She scrunches her nose. "Well, sometimes. Tonight they were screaming. I mean *screaming*! Then Mom takes it out on me, like it's my fault she and Dad can't stand each other. She yells at me about how insensitive I am to have her take me and pick me up, and don't I ever think about her and her needs. I mean, doesn't she mean to say all of that to him? It's not my fault. Plus, I'd drive myself in a second if they hadn't grounded me. I don't want her to chauffeur me around. Tomorrow they'll both just act all nicey-nicey to each other, but no one will apologize to me." She shrugs, but I see her eyes are wet. "It's so juvenile and . . . unfair."

"I'm sorry." I hug her. "You know you can always spend the night at my house to get away."

"Thanks. I might need to tonight. We might also need a cab. It looks like Mom forgot us or is just teaching me a lesson."

The other kids tumble into the back of a silver minivan, leaving us alone in the parking lot.

"Okay," I gush, "on a completely separate note, Noah is so amazingly sweet. It feels so natural to have him next to me and whispering to me. I never really liked boys before . . . not like this, anyway."

"Yeah, we're all a little weirded out, Linds. You haven't dumped him because of the way he ties his shoes or because he has a strange middle name or *anything*." Emma places her palm on my forehead. "You feeling okay?"

I feel anxious and dizzy as I think of Noah's soft mouth brushing my ear.

"There must be something *really* wrong with me." I laugh.

Bzzzzz.

My pocket quivers.

I flip open my phone. It's from Noah.

CYT

CANT W8

I type back.

CHAPTER EIGHT

And kick, kick, kick, kick, fan kick, fan kick, jump together, slap, slap, turn, and roll my head. Now, arm up, lock onto Julia's shoulder, snap my head right, and march, march, march, march. The synthesizers in the song scream. The music is the living pulse of the gym, and the dance team is the blood flowing through its veins. And stag leap, swivel, swivel, up, and touch the ground, hold it, and exhale. Next group does the same while I actually snatch a breath of air. And, one, two, pop up, and pose.

"Better, ladies. Fours, you're a half beat behind the threes on that last sequence. Catch up. Follow Melissa's lead on the fans." Todd, our dance coach, paces back and forth in front of us.

I'm hoping he talks a little longer so I can breathe like a normal person again. My heart races so fast, it feels like it will beat right out of my chest and slide across the floor like a hockey puck. I glance at the clock. Time to go. Two hours of practice and my muscles feel like pudding. I'm starving, and I have a heap of homework tonight.

"Once more. Make it count." Todd turns to the CD player, gives us a millisecond to get in position, and punches the Play button.

I reach inside myself to find the energy to perform the whole routine again. The music lifts me and snaps my limbs from one pose to the next. My smile is genuine. The notes fill me and move me. Adrenaline pushes my body around the gym floor until the last note resonates in the air.

I collapse onto the floor along with half the dance team.

"That's it!" Todd shouts. "See you tomorrow. Nice practice, girls."

Melissa reaches out her hand and pulls me to standing.

"I don't know if I can walk to the back of the gym," she pants. Sweat drips down her freckles.

I wipe the smoldering droplets on my own face before they sting my eyes. "I know *I* can't. That's why I'm going to let you carry me."

She rolls her eyes. We attack our water bottles and take our time stretching in the back of the gym. "Sooo, Emma said you and Noah were cozy at youth group?"

"Yeah." I nod, blushing. "It was . . . wow, completely uncomfortable."

"How do you mean?" Melissa asks.

"Oh, he was great. He is so sweet. It's just the topic was," I lower my voice, "sex, and I was so self-conscious sitting next to him while they talked about all that stuff."

"It's awkward enough talking about that without a guy next to you." Melissa leans over her knee.

"Right. So, Mel, you don't have to tell me, but have you and Beau, you know, I mean not have you done it, but have you talked about it, you know, sex?"

Melissa's flushed face deepens to purple. She looks around and whispers, "Lindsey, we were barely dating in the first place, and then we broke up, and then we got back together. Now, we're kind of off again. His parents won't let him date, even though we see each other at school and stuff during basketball season. We haven't had time to even think about that! We're too busy deciding if we're a couple!" She looks at me sideways. "Have you and Noah talked about it?"

"No! I mean he hasn't even tried anything. Which is great. He's just kissed me, more like little pecks, which I loved. I'd just never really thought about the religious part of abstinence before, and last night really has me thinking." I take a sip of water, so sweet and wet, sliding down my parched throat.

"Which religious part?" Melissa asks, switching legs.

"Well, Pastor Ed, he's the youth pastor at youth group, was saying sex is a gift from God, and He wants us to take care of that gift. I'd never considered that before." I normally don't talk about God with my friends. Not that I avoid it, it just doesn't come up, or maybe I feel uneasy. But I know Melissa goes to church, and it's all so heavy on my brain today. A bead of sweat slides down the side of my nose and drops onto the floor. "It sounds hokey, but it kind of makes sense too."

"Yeah, I guess I thought of the whole thing more as a commandment. You're supposed to wait because that's what the Bible *says*. I never thought about it as what God *wants*." Melissa switches legs. "But abstaining because He wants us to makes more sense, actually."

"Sorry, this is heavy stuff." I roll my eyes as I zip my coat.

"No, it's fine, really fine. It's actually good. I'm glad we can talk about it. I'm glad you talked about it with me. And I guess Beau and I might face the issue someday." Melissa tosses her gym bag on her shoulder.

I let that thought take a ride through my head. Will Noah and I have to face the issue? He's a Christian too. He sat on the couch and heard every word Pastor Ed said, just like I did. He saw that match glowing in the silent room. I know what my stance is.

I want to wait until I'm married. It's the right thing to do.

Pastor Ed mentioned Christian teens wearing purity rings on their ring fingers as a symbol of chastity. I slip my thumb around the vacant space on my left hand. I imagine a shiny silver reminder of my promise to Jesus to stay pure for Him. I'll have to look into it. Kristine would get a kick out of that! I can hear her now: "You know that's your wedding finger?"

"I know." I would keep her gaze.

"So, who did you marry?" She'd laugh, not in an evil way, but in a you're-so-queer way.

"I didn't. It's a purity ring."

"Pure of what?" Kristine would raise an eyebrow.

"You know, I'm saving myself for marriage."

"Why?" Kristine would plop me down on her bed. "That totally hot hockey player is into you. Do you know what you're missing? I bet he'd be fabulous. He's clearly in good shape."

I would hit her with a pillow.

CHAPTER NINE

It's Friday night, and I'm going over to Noah's. I'm nervous and excited and jittery. I've never been to his house. I've never met his parents. Well, I've known who they are for years, from the neighborhood and all, but I've never formally met them and definitely not as Noah's girlfriend.

Noah and I have barely seen each other this week, unless you count sending texts and chatting for a few seconds now and then in the cafeteria. I've had practice every night and he's had practice every morning early—at six o'clock—something about it being impossible to get ice time. He has two away games tomorrow and another one on Sunday. So he won't even be at youth group. This is our only chance to see each other, and I can't wait!

Mom likes that Noah came to our house first. She thinks he's polite. She called his mom on the phone to make sure I was invited and Mr. and Mrs. Hornung would be home. Did I mention I have to meet his parents?

I've thought and rethought my outfit. I want to convey the right message. I'm wearing a coral sweater twin set and these great flared camel-colored cords. I look conservative (for his parents), but pretty (for Noah). My coral and aqua headband pulls my straightened hair from my face. I've decided to grow out my bangs, so they're pulled back too.

I don't mind walking through the neighborhood. I feel like I'm nine again, slipping through yards, trying not to set off any dogs barking, cutting through the right places to avoid fences. The cold air cuts right through my shearling coat. It makes me feel awake and alive. The sky has a pale yellow cast as the day turns to night. It's perfectly silent and the air has the crisp, metallic smell like it might snow.

I take my time, breathing in the dusk. I left the house at 5:55 and don't want to arrive exactly at six, looking overly eager, but I am. I want to hear Noah laugh and have him be next to me and smell his special smell. I also want him to kiss me again, but I have no idea if that'll happen with his 'rents around. I want to charm Mr. and Mrs. Hornung—to make them think I'm the perfect girl for their son.

He's sitting on his front porch as I walk up the driveway. My heart is going up and down like a sewing machine needle.

Noah shrugs in his khaki barn jacket and stands. "Just thought I'd wait for you out here. The stars are coming out."

I look up. In the purplish sky, tiny lights gradually ignite.

"Come on in. It's freezing."

We shuffle into the tan brick split-level. The houses are smaller at this end of the neighborhood, simpler. I like it. I take off my shoes and coat. His house smells like black licorice and roast beef.

Noah leads me into the den, which is a really small, closed-in room, with three hunter green walls and two brown-and-green-plaid love seats piled with cushions. Handles of hockey sticks peek out from behind the couch. The faint odor of smelly feet lingers. A plasma TV is on one wall and a Wii with a tangle of cords covers the floor.

Mr. and Mrs. Hornung sit stiffly on one of the love seats. This room looks like it's been taken over by Noah and his younger brother, Adam.

"Mom, Dad . . ." Noah's fingers weave through his hair. "This is Lindsey. Lindsey, these are my parents."

"It's nice to see you again, Lindsey." His mom smiles at me from her awkward perch. Her dark curls are pulled back out of her face with tortoise shell combs. She looks like an L.L.Bean model with her cardigan and turtleneck.

"Hi, Lindsey. We've heard a lot about you." Mr. Hornung stands and reaches out his hand to shake mine. Noah looks like him, dark and rugged.

I nervously shake his hand and turn to Mrs. Hornung. She's where Noah gets his height. She's at least three inches taller than her husband! "Nice to see you too." I manage.

"It's been awhile since I've seen you riding your scooter around the neighborhood." She smiles.

"I'm just counting down the days until I can drive a car around the neighborhood." I laugh nervously. What have they heard about me? Do they know Noah called me his girlfriend? That he kissed me? Has he had other girls over? Did they like them? I want them to like me. I want to do the right thing, but I'm not sure what that is. I feel awkward. As natural as it is for me to talk to my friends, I can't think of one thing to say to Noah's parents.

"Don't count too quickly." Mr. Hornung smiles. "Now that Noah can drive, we make him run all kinds of errands for us."

"I'd drive you anywhere you wanted too." Noah smiles. "So . . ." Noah rubs his palms together as if he can't get enough Emilio Estevez. "Who's up for *MD2*?"

"Are you really making Lindsey watch that?" his mom asks, rolling her eyes.

"Making?" Noah turns to me. "She loves the Mighty Ducks. Don't you, Linds?"

"How could I not?" I look at Mrs. Hornung for pity.

"Well, between you and Adam, we've seen this one about four thousand times. I won't spoil the ending." Mr. Hornung laughs and leaves the room.

"Have fun," Mrs. Hornung says. "If the movie is too awful, you can always come into the family room and watch TV with us, Lindsey."

"Thanks, Mrs. Hornung." I laugh. "I might need to take you up on that." I like her. I see where Noah gets his ability to make people feel comfortable.

"You at least have to watch all of *MD2*. We're having a double feature you know. *Mighty Ducks 3* is just waiting over here." Noah points to the top of the TV where the DVD case sits and elbows me. His mom smiles as she turns to go.

As soon as we're alone, Noah turns to me. "Want something to drink?"

"No thanks." I shrug and plop onto the love seat.

"They're funny." He shakes his head.

"All parents are." I laugh. "Where's Adam?"

"He's at Colt's house or somewhere. I don't really remember. I just know I finally get you all to myself." He leans toward me and brushes my lips with his just like the other time. He tastes cold and sharp and sweet like the gum I always smell on his breath.

He leans back and looks me right in the eyes. My neck muscles don't seem capable of holding his gaze. There is less than a centimeter separating our faces. Our noses bump, and I laugh.

"Quack, quack, quack." Noah dims the lights and pushes Play.

The movie is on, but I couldn't care less about the kids on ice. I want Noah to kiss me again. I listen to his breathing. His fingers reach out and curl around mine. It's dark like a real movie theater in here. He wiggles my fingers slightly, like a tickle. I feel his thigh against mine. A few minutes later he leans into my ear and whispers, "Are you ready for a drink yet?"

I turn to answer, but when I do my face is in his face. I bite my lip. I shake my head, but his mouth is on my mouth, and we're kissing, and his hands slide on my back, holding me close to him. I feel like I'm flying, and he's warm and intoxicating. He leans his chest against mine, so I'm sandwiched between the couch and Noah, like a piece of paper slid under a paperweight, protected from the wind so I won't blow away. And we kiss and we kiss and we kiss, and his lips are warm and wet, and his hands slide under my T-shirt to the small of my back. They feel like fire against my skin. I hear footsteps, and I pull back to end the kiss but end up embedding myself in a jumble of couch cushions.

Noah must hear the footsteps too.

He exhales. "Wow." He shakes himself and stands.

I'm breathing more heavily than when I finish a dance routine.

"I'll go get some Gatorade." Noah's cheeks are flushed as he walks out of the room.

"You two doing okay?" I hear Mrs. Hornung ask him in the kitchen.

I'm thankful for a moment to myself. I sit up as straight as I can and smooth out my cardigan. I retuck my top into my cords. My headband is around my neck. I slide it back into place and bob my knee up and down as I look around the room. I'm disoriented. I've never felt anything like that in my life. I turn the dimmer switch to full wattage to snap myself out of my reverie. How long were we kissing? I have no idea what's going on in the movie, and I have to go to the bathroom. I wish Noah were back. I feel conspicuously alone in his house. What if one of his parents walks in? What would I say? Would they know what we've been doing? I try to watch the movie but can't focus my eyes or thoughts. My brain teems with mouths and heat and Noah's weight against me.

"I thought I'd grab some chips and salsa too. Why don't you push Pause and keep me company in the kitchen?" Noah's silhouette fills the doorway.

I jump at his voice. "Sure." I fumble for the remote and press Pause, not able to think of anything funny or coy as a reply. What do you say to someone after they've kissed you like that?

"Actually, could you show me where the bathroom is?"

"Right down there." Noah points down the hall.

"Thanks." I walk into the burgundy powder room and close the door. A grouping of three paintings of wild ducks hangs on the wall, and ducks are embroidered into the beige towels. It's so dark and men's-clubbish. I laugh. I guess decor is a little different when it's three guys and one girl in the house, versus our three girls and Dad. I look in the mirror. I expect my image to betray my kissing frenzy. But my hair isn't mussed, and except for my bare lips where my lip gloss has been smooched, I look pretty normal. I use the restroom, extremely conscious of the noise of the flushing toilet and the faucet as I wash my hands with a bar of lemon-and-thyme-scented soap. I reapply the lip gloss I had safely stashed in my pocket and take a deep breath. I'm starting to feel normal again.

Ta tatatat ta! The friendly sound of chips tumbling into a bowl fills the fluorescent-lighted kitchen. Noah's mom chats on the phone and smiles at me, then turns and walks out with the white cordless.

"Would you grab the salsa?" Noah asks, motioning to a jar on the counter. "I've always loved this movie," he says, carrying the bowl of chips and a tall glass with ice clanking against its sides back into the den, "but I don't remember it being sooo . . ." He stops and turns so that he's directly in front of me. "Exciting." He playfully nips at my lips, the quickest kiss, and then another and another as if he's going for the world's record for fastest consecutive kisses.

I laugh out loud and fall back into the couch. I'm relieved he doesn't revert the lighting back to the secretive dusk. We watch the rest of the movie and the next one too with our heads at separate ends of the couch and our stocking feet entwined with each other. We giggle and chat and play footsie while the Mighty Ducks win yet another championship game.

"I'll walk you home." Noah shoves his hands in his pockets.

"Great." All of a sudden I'm exhausted. My eyelids fight to stay open.

We walk the long way home along the sidewalks, under the streetlights around to my house. The crisp air gives me a second wind.

"So, three games this weekend?" I ask.

"Yeah, the other team's decent, but we're better. We should win if we keep our heads on straight."

"I wish I could come." I watch his Nikes slap the cement.

"These are too far away." He slips off my mitten and weaves his fingers in mine. "Next week, we're home."

"Cool. I'll have to perform at the basketball game on Friday, but I could come on Saturday. Do you play on Saturday?" I ask, feeling stupid for not knowing his schedule.

"You won't miss anything on Friday. We have the night off. And yes, always on Saturdays."

We walk in silence for a few minutes, but it's not awkward. For once, I'm not scanning my head for conversation. I'm just enjoying the warmth of his hand on mine, the sound of our footsteps, and the idea that I'm Noah's girlfriend.

When we reach my house, he stops before I can climb the three steps to my front porch. Our outside house light streams on us like a spotlight.

"I burned a CD for you." He slides a disc out of his jacket like a magician.

I reach out for the circle, as if it's an enchanted stone or a magic wand and I'm sizing up its powers.

"Thanks."

His lips are on mine again, and not for just a second this time. They linger and hold my lips. Just as I feel all warm and giddy, he pulls away.

"I'll watch you in."

I can't speak. He keeps taking me by surprise. Surprised by his kiss, surprised by his pulling away, surprised by the CD, surprised by his finality of the evening. I feel like I'm in a Ping-Pong match watching the ball go back and forth, from him being as nervous and excited as I am to him being totally in control. Thank goodness he is, because I am not. I'm not in control at all.

"Good luck tomorrow." I smile.

"Thanks, Linds. G'night."

"Good night." Ten feet separates us, now twenty, now I'm touching my door, and he's standing like a statue, watching over me.

I play the CD while I get ready for bed. The first song is "Hey There Delilah" by the Plain White T's. I sit on the edge of my bed, absorbing every note and word as if Noah were serenading me. Tomorrow, I'll load it onto my computer and update my iPod. I brush my teeth to "Perfect" by the Smashing Pumpkins. I wash my face to "I've Just Seen a Face" sung by Jim Sturgess. I turn down the volume way low, so I can drift into my dreams as Lenny Kravitz chants "I'll Be Waiting."

CHAPTER TEN

My dream state lingers all week. I listen to the songs Noah burned over and over again, as if he's burned them into my heart. They're intense and full of passion.

"I still can't believe he made this for me," I tell my friends over lunch on Friday.

"Sounds like true love," Emma growls, not even looking up from her nachos. "Do ya think we could talk about something other than Noah? Anything?"

Ouch. I feel like I've nicked myself shaving.

Raven must also feel the sting in Emma's remark. "Seriously, Linds. He's really into you. Everyone knows Noah isn't like this for girls."

I swish her words around in my mouth. I have so many questions about that comment. Like, what girls isn't he like this for? Were there other girls who were into him, but he didn't fall for? Has he told the hockey team I'm his girlfriend? Does Raven know because Randy's told her? It sounds like it when she uses words like "everyone."

I don't want to sound stupid, so I just ask, "Like what?"

"You know, all Romeo. It's not like you're the first girl to like *him*. The team would die if they knew he made you a CD." Raven dips one of Emma's chips into the neon orange cheese sauce. "But, you're the first girl he likes back."

I'm so nervous inside it's hard to remember to eat. I look at the slice of pizza on my tray with only one bite taken out of it. I nod and take a big bite, but as I chew I wonder where Noah is in the cafeteria and if he wonders where I am.

Peter lumbers over with Randy, who thwaps Raven in the head with a notebook.

"Ouch." She turns and sticks her tongue out at him.

Two strong arms circle me from behind.

"I know you're coming to my game tomorrow, so I thought I'd come to the basketball game tonight and watch you dance." Noah's lips brush against my ear as he whispers.

My face feels as hot as if it were directly under one of those air dryers in the ladies' room.

"And the dance after the game?" I ask, hanging the question I've been contemplating all week in the air.

"The dance?" Noah releases me, chomps a bite of my pizza, and then hands it to me. "You mean, here in the cafeteria? That dance? Do you girls dance?" he asks the table.

"Darlin', you haven't seen anything until you've seen *us* dance." Melissa, who's usually so quiet, lights up when it comes to dancing. I love that about her!

"Y'all have gotta be better than Peter and Noah." Randy laughs. "These boys can't feel the beat."

"Sounds like we'll have to have a dance contest." Gracie smiles.

"I'm in, but just as a judge." Noah laughs. "I'll leave the cha-cha-cha-ing up to you!" He pecks me on the cheek and stands up. "See ya tonight, ladies." He winks and walks away with his friends.

My skin tingles, like I've just applied astringent on my face.

"See ya tonight, ladies," Emma echoes in a high-pitched nasally voice.

I don't know why she's being cruel, but I can't take it. "What's up, Em? Something bugging you?"

"Yeah, Miss Perfect. It may be all well and good that Prince Charming is singing you love songs and ready to dance with you at the royal ball, but it's not like that for all of us ugly stepsisters."

My anger turns to confusion. "Em?" I ask. The rest of the table is silent. Emma and I go way back. This is our battle.

Emma slouches in her chair with her eyes averted to the floor.

"Em?" I ask again. She doesn't answer. "First of all, you are *not* an ugly stepsister. You are beautiful and talented, and I would kill for your hair! Secondly, if you don't speak, Ariel, we'll never know which prince you want to dance with."

Emma's lips curl in the slightest smile. She always pretended she was the Little Mermaid when we were little. Her eyes, however, stay focused on the dingy floor.

"Well, Peter is fairly cute, and I thought we kind of hit it off when the two of us defaulted on your and Noah's parade," she spits out the real issue, then shrugs. Fire creeps across her pale skin to match her hair.

"You like Peter!" Raven practically screams.

Emma rolls her eyes.

"Okay, girls." Gracie steps in. "This is the deal." She shifts her gaze around the table to recruit us into her plan. "We need to get Emma and Peter alone at the dance. Peter's kind of quiet, and he always seems glued to Noah." Gracie narrows her black eyes. "So, let's push Lindsey and Noah together and off to the side. That gives Linds some time with her new flame, but more importantly, by getting Noah away from the crowd, it will give us a chance to nudge Peter toward Emma. It at least gives them a shot." She wiggles her lower jaw back and forth. "Melissa, Raven, and I have to forfeit our own love lives — at least until we get Peter to dance with you, Emma."

"What love life?" Raven picks up the remains of her lunch and takes it over to the trash can.

"Poor, Rav." I sigh dramatically. "The most athletic, exotic beauty in school with the enchanting drawl of a Southern belle. We really feel sorry for you." I place my arm across my face in mock pity.

"Well, someone has to get the scholarships and play for the Olympic team." Raven flashes a huge smile. "I guess it's all about sacrifice, just like Scarlett O'Hara." She sits back down at the table.

"Okay, Miss O'Hara." Melissa giggles at Raven, then turns to the rest of us. "We need a plan."

"We have to sit with the dance team for the first half of the game. We perform at halftime." I take a sip of Diet Coke. "Mel and I can meet up with you during the second half, but I'll need a major shower and primp session before the dance."

"After third quarter we'll hit the locker room." Melissa nods.

"What are you wearing?" Gracie asks.

"I have this completely wild top I tricked my dad into paying for." Emma leans back in her chair.

The bell rings. I love my friends, but I think I might really love Noah. In the middle of lunch in front of all the school, did he really put his arms around me? Did he really just take a bite of my pizza? Only people in my family do that! The dance is just hours away, and I have to perform before then.

CHAPTER ELEVEN

Beep beep beep.
I open the microwave and pull out my leftover pasta. Kristine walks into the kitchen smelling like an ashtray.

"Make some for me, too?" she asks.

"Sure. What time do you have to be at the game?"

"I don't know. Six?" She stretches in a big yawn, which somehow accentuates her perfect body. "You?"

"Not until six thirty for inspection. We have to be in the gym at seven when the varsity game starts." I open the microwave, pull out my pasta, and put a plate in for Kristine. "Are you going to the dance?"

"Mom thinks I am." Kristine plops on a barstool and clanks a fork on the counter. "But I think Wes and I are going to find a place to be alone. You know?"

"Mmmm." I nod, keeping my back to her. I can guess what they'll do in their alone space, wherever that is. I think of Noah's body pressing against mine on his couch. I flash to Pastor Ed's match. I feel woozy.

"How are things with your hotshot hockey player?" Steam pours over Kristine's face as she lifts the plastic wrap from her plate. It veils her expression.

"Good." I can't conceal my grin. I sit down next to her and

taste a bite of pasta layered with tangy artichokes and sundried tomatoes. "We're meeting at the dance."

"I know it's kind of weird to talk about . . ." Kristine looks at me. "But if you're going to sleep with him or if you already are, you really need to use protection."

"I'm not going to—it's not, it's not like that," I stammer. My face feels enveloped in steam too, but not from my pasta.

"Alright." Kristine shrugs. "If I were you, I'd want to get my hands all over that hot hockey bod. But when it *is* like that, let me know. I'll help you get what you need. Okay?"

I know Kristine is trying to be big sisterly and look out for me. She's clearly not waiting until she's married. Is Wes the right guy for her? Why and when did she decide to give up her virginity to him? Or did she sleep with someone else before him? I'm half-tempted to ask her what sex is like, but then I envision Ed's fire and say a quick prayer under my breath. *Dear God, please keep Kristine from getting burned.* I feel the invisible imprints Noah's hands left on my back and stand to get a fork.

"Okay," I answer.

/ / /

At school I rush into the music room with a plate of brownies. The thick cloud of aerosol hairspray and boot polish makes me cough.

"Wow, the Barbie doll brought in brownies," Jill announces to the team. I bite my tongue. It's not worth snapping back at her.

Girls crowd around the plate and thank me. I grab two brownies and scan the room for Melissa. She's in the corner, zipping her boots.

"Hey." She smiles.

"Want one?" I ask, holding out a brownie.

"No thanks. If there are any left, I'll have one afterward." She switches feet. "My luck, I'd get brownie all over my uniform and not pass inspection."

I look over to the swarm. "The odds of you getting one afterward look slim." I smile, but I don't want to push her. Melissa has enough issues with food. She doesn't need me complicating things for her. The rich fudgy smell wafting from the napkin is too enticing for me. I take a gooey, chocolaty bite.

"Mmmmmm. So . . ." I finish chewing my brownie. "I've been in such a rush to get dressed and polish my boots and iron and bake, I'm a little nervous." I place my hand on my chest. "I can't get my heart to slow down."

"Take deep breaths." Mel leans over and hugs me. "We still have five minutes until Todd shows up, and you are completely ready. Your hair looks darling, of course."

"Thanks." I smile. I inhale and exhale and close my eyes for just a minute, facing Melissa, so none of the other girls think I'm nutty. I'm so jittery. I don't like this feeling.

Slow down, a voice says inside my head. *Talk to Me. Melissa understands.*

God always pops in when I need Him. I feel awkward saying this to Melissa, but I think I'm supposed to.

"How about we pray?" I ask.

Melissa nods and holds out her hands. Even in her gloves, her fingers feel like icicles.

"Dear Jesus, please help us to do our best out there tonight. Help our dancing and everything we do serve You. Amen."

"Amen," Melissa echoes. "That was great, Linds. I don't know why I never thought to pray before."

"I don't know. It just came to me." I feel better. I'm less shaky and more relaxed. "I have another idea." I smile. "Let's trade our gloves for good luck."

"You're kooky." Melissa rolls her eyes, but starts pulling the white gloves we wear to perform off her spindly fingers.

"Well, Kristine says the cheerleaders trade pompoms for good luck. Why can't we have our own thing?"

"I like it." She smiles.

I tug on her gloves. The extra fabric to accommodate her elongated fingers flaps at the end of my hands. Meanwhile she tugs on my petite pair, and they don't quite cover her hands. We start giggling as Todd opens the doors.

Clap! Clap! Clap!

"Inspection in ten, nine, eight, seven, six, five, four, Stacey, where are you, blow your whistle, three, two, one."

Our captain, Stacey, jumps to attention and tweets her silver whistle, sending a shrill signal through the room. We hurl ourselves into line, standing at attention with our arms flat against our sides, our shoulders rolled back, our chins in the air, and our feet in third position, right heels imbedded in left insteps.

The room is silent except for our heavy breathing and Todd's shoes slowly creeping past each of us, pausing to ensure we are immaculate and identical.

"Jill, more hairspray, you have some flyaways." He inches down the line. I sense it, even though I don't dare look. We're not even supposed to move our eyes.

"Katie, your heels need a touch-up."

"Melissa, a little flair in the hair. Lindsey, help her."

Tweet tweet tweet tweet. "Dismissed," Stacey bellows.

"You have fifteen minutes to fix your flaws and hit the ladies' room. We'll line up at precisely 6:55 p.m." Todd meanders to the brownies. "Yummmmmy!" he says, sampling one. "My compliments to the cook."

"Lindsey brought 'em," J.T. mumbles, but I'm on to Melissa's hair.

"I hate getting singled out." Even Melissa's freckles are blushing.

"It's all right. Come on, I have an extra bow."

CHAPTER TWELVE

We sit with the pep band behind the basketball players for the first half of the game. I spot Noah on the other side of the gym in the student section. He and a bunch of his buddies are all wearing their hockey jerseys and goofing around. I struggle to make eye contact. He seems too into his friends to notice me. And then it's halftime.

We line up beside the bleachers and march into the middle of the gymnasium floor. Our boots echo like playground balls bouncing as we parade in front of the stands. We strike our opening pose and wait.

Boom boom boom! Everything comes alive. The sound system blares our music, and we kick and lean and jump and snap. I am the music, and I am a smile, and my heart beats with the music, and there is no Noah or crowd or Kristine to worry about or outfits to pick out or homework to finish or Dad to miss. Then it's over. The music stops, and we freeze, smiles plastered to our faces. Sweat dribbles from my forehead down my fiery face. My insides feel like an erupting volcano. My heartbeat is the lava trying to push out and overflow.

Tweet tweet tweet tweet. We obey the whistle's commands and march out of the gym. Once we're past the eyes of the audience, we melt and hug and cheer. Melissa and I run to the girls' room.

I splash cold water on my face, trying to bring down my body temp.

"That was awesome!" I exclaim.

"We totally nailed that routine." Melissa wipes her face with a paper towel. "I think it's the first time we got the timing on the fan perfect." She slurps water from the faucet. "Ready?"

Raven and Emma sit in their usual spot. Unfortunately it's rows and rows away from Noah.

"Where's Gracie?" Melissa asks, scooching next to Emma on the bleachers.

"She went to get a snack with Drew." Emma slides over to make room for us.

"We're winning!" Raven says, keeping her eyes trained on the court. "Beau just scored, Mel!"

Melissa squeals and claps her hands.

I try not to look where Noah's sitting. If he wants to find me, he can. I pay extra attention to my friends and laugh extra hard at their stories. I don't want him to think I'm needy, and I do love my friends. But there's a pit in my stomach.

Just like we planned, Melissa and I shower after third quarter. I hate showering in the communal locker room with my loofah on a metal peg outside the flimsy white curtain. It smells like rust and Clorox. I cringe as my bare feet trek across the slippery floor where hundreds of unknown feet have trod. It's even worse, once I'm clean, and I'm forced to retrace my steps across the slimy tiles.

Luckily, I have lots to distract me—mostly Noah, and how I want to look perfect for him tonight. He didn't notice me at the game, but he will at the dance. After sliding my flatiron through my hair and then through Melissa's, I shellac the last coat of shimmer on my lips.

We leave the locker room and head to the darkened cafeteria.

HOT

The room is heavy with sweat and perfume. All the tables and chairs have been stacked against the walls to create a makeshift dance floor. A DJ is set up near the lunch line, and neon lights flash from his sound system.

"Did they say where they'd meet us?" Melissa shouts over the blaring tunes.

I bop my head to the music. "No! I'll text Em." I whip out my fuchsia phone and type.

WHERE R U

Melissa and I meander around the perimeter jammed with jumping, swaying, and stomping students — a sea of jeans and hair and sweat. My legs itch to dance and jam, but we have to find our friends first. A minute later my phone vibrates in my pocket.

BY BLU LOX

"They're by the blue lockers." I grab Melissa's hand and drag her though the crowd. "This way!"

Gracie is all smiles, swaying near Drew, Emma's practicing her head banging, red curls flying everywhere, and Raven is doing some slick move with her perfectly toned body.

"I have *got* to learn how to do that!" I grab Raven's elbow.

"Hi, guys!" Melissa yells.

I wave to everyone and focus on imitating Raven. Soon she has me swiveling my hips and moving my arms like hers.

"This one's my favorite!" Raven squeals when the song we're dancing to morphs into another tune.

I practice the move she taught me and blend it with some of my own. I edge over to Melissa, coaxing her to do it with me. A strong warm arm pulls me close. I know it's him without looking.

"Okay, so you girls really can dance!" Peter shouts, grabbing Emma's hand and twirling her around. I cheer inside for Emma. Peter's usually so quiet.

Noah leans over and kisses my cheek. He smells like mint, but also of beer. So that's why Peter's so outgoing tonight. I didn't know Noah drank. The print of his lips on my cheek tingles.

"You look awesome!" Noah whispers in my ear as he pulls his lips away. "How'd I get such a hot girlfriend?"

My insides feel like a bottle of nail polish being shaken to mix the color. Upside down: I'm disgusted that Noah drinks. I mean, lots of people at school do; I just didn't know he did. It caught me off guard, and, well, I'm disappointed. Right side up: I'm excited. I love it when Noah calls me his girlfriend, and I'm giddy that he thinks I'm hot. I wouldn't want him to think I was dumpy or plain or even just "cute." I'm relieved he came to find me. I was a little worried about his lack of attention during the game. I feel angry and happy all at once. Luckily, I don't have to say a word. No one's talking—just jamming.

We dance and dance. My heart pumps so fast I feel like there's not enough oxygen in the crowded cafeteria for my lungs.

"I need some air!" I scream at Noah. He nods and takes my hand. We're not allowed to leave the cafeteria and then reenter the dance—school rules. So he pulls me to the back of the cafeteria near one of the stacks of tables. He leans me against the wall and kisses me full on the lips. It's like I lit a sparkler. The colors whirl around me. I pull away.

"Sorry, Charlie. No PDA. Dance team rules." I pant, shaking my finger at him like a child walking through the house with muddy shoes.

"What's PDA?" Noah asks. "And who's Charlie? Should I be jealous?"

"Funny!" I slap him playfully on the arm. "Public Display of Affection." I inhale some fresh air, relieved to be out of the mob for a moment. "Todd, our coach, assigns demerits to anyone caught in the act of PDA — enough that I'd have to skip a performance."

"Demerits?" Noah asks, leaning in to kiss my ear.

"Yeah, points against us." I playfully push him away. "You know, like if we forget part of our uniform or are late to practice. It's a point system of punishment." He's still looking at me like I have fifteen purple eyes. "Like in hockey, what happens if you forget your stick or you're late?"

"If you forget your stick? You better not forget your stick! If you're late? Either way, it's a bunch of nasty drills, like sprints on the ice." He shrugs. "I get it." He takes his forearm and wipes sweat from his brow. His cheeks are rosy, and he is so handsome that I want him to kiss me like that again and again.

"So, no kissing in school?"

I nod.

"So, where can we go so I can kiss you?" he asks in a voice so low I barely hear him.

"I can't leave the dance. My mom's picking us up." I smile, somewhat relieved. What would happen if we left together? Wow, is he cute!

He shakes his head all nervous like. "Linds, you look so sexy, and you go dancing like that, and you expect me to keep my hands off you?" He ruffles his hair. "This isn't easy."

"I'm sorry. I want to kiss you. That was so . . . niiiiccce." I draw out the word and tilt my head sideways. I don't want him to think I'm not interested. "But, I guess it's kind of like what Ed was talking about. Even though it feels good, some things are just against the rules, whether they're Todd's or God's." I laugh at my unintentional rhyme. "And, it's not worth it. I mean, can you imagine if you couldn't play tomorrow because someone saw you kiss me? That's what would it would be like for me."

Noah steps back. "I never thought of it that way, Linds." He grabs my hand and stands next to me, shoulder to shoulder. "I'm sorry. I really am. I didn't mean to put you in that position." His free hand fidgets with his hair. "You're just so amazing, and I think about you all the time."

"I think about you too," I say.

"Really?"

"Noah!" I punch him in the arm. "Of course, like always. I was so bummed my friends weren't sitting near you at the game, and I picked out this outfit because I hoped you would like it, and I can still feel where you kissed me." The words tumble out of my mouth too fast.

"About the game . . ." Noah looks down. "The guys all went out drinking before, and I had a beer—one beer. I feel so stupid. I didn't want you to think I was into drinking or anything, so I avoided you during the game, hoping they'd sober up and I wouldn't stink." He turns and looks at me. "You were great out there, by the way. I am so crazy about you, Lindsey Kraus."

My smile explodes from my heart. "Me, you." I squeeze his hand. Wow! I am so blown away by him. I want him to realize how much I like him too, but I'm agitated. I don't want this to go in the wrong direction. Dance team and demerits are one reason to slow things down, but there's more.

"Noah, I love kissing you, and the other night at your house—wow! That threw me over the top. But, remember what Pastor Ed said about the fire. I mean, I can't go *there*."

I watch Noah's Adam's apple bob up and down. "Sure, Linds. I get it." He swallows again. "Wow, will it be hard, because you're so gorgeous and, don't get me wrong, so much more. I mean, I love being with you, because you're you and the gorgeous part is just a bonus." He squeezes my hand tightly.

Good thing it's dark in here, so he can't see me blushing.

"I mean I've done it before. It's not like if we don't, I'll get hazed by the hockey team for still being a virgin. That's not why I'm in this, Linds. You're great. I don't ever want to do anything you're uncomfortable with."

The flip-flops are back. He agrees. He respects me. He's sorry. He *loves* being with me. He didn't actually say he loved me, but it was close, wasn't it? He's not a virgin!

"You've done it before!" I feel stretched like a face from the comics imprinted on a piece of Silly Putty, taut and distorted.

Noah nods, not like this is a big confession, just a fact, like he told me what number's on his jersey.

"Who . . . ?" I start to ask, but can't finish my sentence because my mouth will not close from this *o* shape.

"Isabelle Parker." He shrugs.

"Isabelle Parker!" I scream. Isabelle is tall, dark, and curvy with thick black eyelashes. She is my polar opposite. I think of my chest so flat that I can buy clothes from the kids' department. She could be in the *Sports Illustrated* swimsuit edition with her measurements, and she dresses so everyone at school knows it. I instantly hate her. Just like that. One minute ago, she was just another student—someone whose name I knew and nothing else. Now she's the enemy. She and Noah shared something that he and I have never shared. What did he see in her? Well, other than the obvious.

"Did you guys go out?" I ask. I couldn't remember them being an item. Hadn't he said he'd never had a girlfriend before? Or did Gracie say that? Or Raven?

"It doesn't matter." Noah places his amazingly soft, warm hand on my cheek. "It doesn't matter at all. I didn't even know you, Linds. It's you I'm crazy about. Not her."

CHAPTER THIRTEEN

I'm in my room, flipping through magazines while I commiserate with Gracie via texting, because Drew and Noah have away games again all weekend. It's Saturday morning, the day before Valentine's Day. Not much of a romantic weekend!

It's been a week since the dance. I've had time to roll this thing about Noah around and around in my head. I've prayed about it. Jesus says to forgive and not to judge, and I'm really trying to do that. And by the way, Noah's right: He didn't even know me when he slept with Isabelle. He didn't cheat on *me*. Still, every time I pass Isabelle in the halls, I cringe. But, then, Noah is so cute and funny and never mentions other girls or even pays attention to them, unless you count hanging with my friends. He is a Christian, right? Why and when did he decide not to wait until marriage? But Noah makes me happy — so happy. And he isn't pressuring me at all. So, for now, all is good, well mostly.

"Knock, knock," Mom says from the hallway, even though my door's open.

G2G

I text to Gracie and click my phone shut.

"What's up?" I ask Mom.

"Noah's here." Mom smiles a mischievous smile.

"Aaagh!" I scream. I know why Mom's smiling. I'm still

wearing my pj's, and I'm not wearing a drop of makeup.

"How long can you stall him?" I ask.

"Well, I'm cute." Mom winks. "But I don't think he came to see me."

"Right." I tug off my flannel pants and jump into a pair of jeans wadded up at the foot of my bed. Thankfully, my lilac hoodie is clean and sitting on my dresser in a stack of folded clothes. I pull it over my cami and rush to the bathroom before my head even pops through the neck hole. I brush my teeth and wash my face in record time and settle with mascara and lip gloss. The whole process takes about three minutes.

"Hey." I smile, trying not to sound out of breath as I walk down the stairs. Noah stands in the hallway all mussed, like he just crawled out of bed.

"Hey." He pecks me on the cheek. He still smells of sleep and covers. I want to cozy up next to him. "What are you doing?" he asks.

"Nothing. Didn't Mom invite you in?"

"I was hoping to convince you to come out."

"Where? I thought you were out of town?"

"It's a surprise." His cheeks flush. "We got back late, and we're leaving in three hours to go back. Coach decided at the last minute not to stay in Ackley overnight."

I bite my bottom lip. I wasn't expecting to see him today and wondered if Valentine's meant anything to him, and here he is at my house with a secret plan!

"I already checked with your Mom, and she's okay. You game?"

"Sure, what should I wear?"

He rolls his eyes. "Look at me, Linds. Does it look like it matters?"

"Am I okay, really?"

"Really. But grab a coat and gloves and maybe a hat." He looks down at my feet. "You'll need taller socks. No footies allowed."

"Right." I laugh.

"No, seriously," he says.

I don't have a clue where he's taking me, but I do know a hat will ruin anything decent I have going on with my hair. Agh, who cares?!

"Just a sec." I giggle as I trot into the kitchen.

"Mom, Noah says you're okay if we go somewhere?"

"Have fun." Mom smiles knowingly while mushing ground beef into meatballs. The smell of the spices she's mixing fill the kitchen and tickle my nose.

"You know where we're going, don't you?" I march right up next to her.

"Yup." She looks down at the meaty mess. "But I'm not telling." She gives a fake twang. "Just go, or I'll have to touch you!" Mom holds up her fingers dripping with ground beef.

"Ahhh!" I scream and dart to the closet. I pull on my puffy coat with the cute faux-fur-lined hood and my cream knit mittens and hat. I sprint up the stairs and grab a pair of socks and my UGGs. As soon as I have them on, I spring back down. I shrug as I take a quick glance in the hall mirror.

"Ready," I announce back in the foyer.

Noah puts his gloved hand in my mittened one as we traipse through the neighborhood. Maybe he's taking me to his house. I hope there's not a *Mighty Ducks 4*. But we don't go that way. We head toward the big field fringed by corkscrew willows that separates our subdivision from the next one. Whoever owns the land won't sell, so it remains untouched and wild.

"Wow, I haven't been out here in forever." I sigh. "I used to catch frogs, climb trees, pretend I was on secret missions, all kinds of stuff out here."

"I think everyone in the neighborhood used it as an escape. I love this place." Noah squeezes my hand. "Well, here we are." We're standing on the edge of the pond frozen over with thick, dark green ice. Noah walks behind a tree stump and pulls out two pairs of ice skates.

"Sit down, Cinderella. Let me put on your glass slippers."

"We're skating?" He must have planned everything. He stashed the skates here. He set things up with Mom.

"I want to share this with you," Noah whispers.

I can't answer. My emotions are stuck in a thick, gooey ball in my throat. I know skating means everything to him. I sit obediently and let him lace my skates. When they're tied he laces his own.

"Ready." He takes my hand.

The cold, metallic scraping of skates on ice echoes through the vacant field. It's just Noah and me. He faces me and holds my hands, skating backward as we make our way slowly around the pond.

"I didn't know anyone skated out here." My words seem too loud for this peaceful, private spot.

"It's where I learned." Snow shavings fly from Noah's left skate as he flips his ankles to a stop. "Ice time is expensive, and the rink's always packed. So, on days I didn't have hockey, I'd come out here and practice and practice and practice." His voice trails off as he leans forward to kiss me. His lips are warm and sweet.

"I love you, Lindsey. Happy Valentine's Day." His emerald eyes peek through his thick lashes.

I feel like I'm in a movie. I can't remember ever being this happy.

"I love you, too." I hadn't said it out loud to my friends or even to myself, but I knew it was true. The words had bubbled at my lips a couple of times, but I didn't want him to think I was clingy and way too into him. Noah saying it first means everything.

He kisses me again, just quick and soft then pulls my hands to keep skating. He doesn't say anything about what we've confessed. As always, it seems so natural with him.

The only interruption of the *swish, swish* of our skates is birds chirping in the branches of the willow trees that hang so low they tickle the frozen ground. "You getting chilly?" Noah asks.

I want to lie and say no. I never want to leave this magical spot, but I feel like a human Popsicle. "I'm freezing." My teeth chatter as I form the words.

We go back to the bumpy log and unlace our skates. Noah pulls out a thermos. He unscrews the top and pours steaming cocoa into the red plastic lid that doubles as a cup. It's sweet and warm and creamy going down, and helps thaw my insides, but I'm still shivering.

"We've got to get you back." Noah laughs. "You're like Karen in *Frosty the Snowman*, remember? In the refrigerated boxcar?"

I laugh. "Only, you're much cuter than Frosty." I kiss Noah's cheek.

Inside my front door I stamp my feet in an effort to shake off the chill.

"Let's go beg Dad to make a fire." I grab Noah's hand. "He's actually in town!"

"I'd love to, Linds, but I've got a game. I really have to get going."

I know he has a game, but I'm crushed. I don't want him to leave. *I love him!*

"I'm really sorry." He leans over and holds me. "I wanted to do something with you for Valentine's. Something special." Every inch of my body is against a part of him. My shivers cease. I love him even more for hugging me, instead of trying to make out. His lips brush mine for an instant, then he whispers it again: "I love you."

"Hang on a minute!" I remember the valentine I have for him in my room. I fly upstairs, grab the package in pink tissue paper with the card taped on top. I run as fast as I can back down the steps and arrive at the bottom, out of breath.

"For you." I catch some air. "It's nothing, compared to what you gave me."

"What is it?" he asks and raises his eyebrows.

"You can open." I nod.

He reads the card, laughs, then gives me a quick kiss. He shreds the beautifully wrapped package as only a guy could do. "Yum!" he declares and grabs one of the brownies with bittersweet frosting I made for him. Then he takes the frame I painted to look like his hockey uniform at Emma's mom's pottery place. He runs his fingertips over the picture of us taken at youth group a couple of weeks ago.

"You are so gorgeous." He shakes his head.

"I love you." I reach up to ruffle that fabulous hair. "Thank you for the best Valentine's ever."

"It is the best. I love this pic." He grins, one side of his mouth creeping up more than the other. He's on the step when I remember.

"Good luck tonight."

"Thanks."

And he's gone.

CHAPTER FOURTEEN

"And swivel, swivel to the left." Todd's voice booms over the music in the church gym.

"Swivel, swivel to the right, swivel, swivel all day and night." Todd breaks out into hysterical laughter, grabs me around the waist and dips me, like Fred Astaire. I am caught completely off guard and have to wiggle and stumble to stop myself from falling flat on my back. Todd's laughter is contagious. I can't breathe, laughing this hard in a backbend.

"Enough ladies." He expertly rolls me up his arm, like a rag doll, into standing position.

"Enough for today. Enjoy your weekend." He doubles over, still laughing.

"Thanks for the dance." I bow toward him.

He smiles his mischievous smile, then flies to the jam box. I have no idea how his body moves like that, like a marionette on strings, effortless, soft and flouncy.

"I secretly admit I'm relieved the basketball team's away tonight." Melissa wipes her sweaty forehead with a towel. "I don't have enough energy to perform!"

"I am so glad, because it means you guys are spending the night! I'm so psyched!" I swallow half my Evian in one gulp. It's been a week now since Valentine's Day, and while I'm still reeling in romance, I am really looking forward to a night with just the girls. "Come on." I grab Melissa's arm, barely allowing her to gather her things and tug on her coat. I hustle her to the parking lot where Mom's Prius is just arriving.

"Did you get out early?" Mom looks puzzled as we scurry into the car.

"No, just ready to party." I smile, reaching for the volume on the stereo. I punch the station to Air1 and crank it up. Melissa and I dance the best we can while buckled. Mom laughs.

"What time's everyone else coming?" Melissa shouts over the stereo.

I turn down the volume to answer, "Around six. That gives us time to shower and change and . . ." I look hopefully to Mom. "Order pizza."

"I already said you could order two pizzas." She smiles.

"And, we can pour the M&M's in bowls and maybe sample half a bag or so until the other girlies ding-dong." Ick! Why'd I say that? I always talk about food; I forget Melissa struggles so much with eating. She's great, though. She just rolls with it.

"Sounds great." Melissa bobs her head.

/ / /

Emma, Raven, Gracie, Melissa, and I lounge in the family room. Plates with half-eaten pizza crusts and bowls with melted puddles of ice cream litter the coffee table. The plasma TV is on, the lights are low, and Raven's got the clicker. She pauses on MTV.

"Isn't that Scarlett Johansson?" Emma asks.

"Yeah, I think so." I examine her pouty lips and curvy body. "Why do you think a big actress like her would do a video?"

"Because it's with Justin Timberlake is why." Gracie unrolls her sleeping bag.

We all sit mesmerized by the music and the dancing and the hoops and the flames and Scarlett's lips and Justin's hands. I feel squirmy and uncomfortable. I mean it's just a video, not some X movie or something, but wow!

"Wow!" Raven passes the clicker to Melissa. "That makes me feel naughty."

I'm glad I'm not the only one. Ever since the incident on Noah's couch, I've had temptations I didn't even know existed. As a Christian, especially one who's saving herself, I know they're all wrong, and I've tried to ignore them. But this sultry video makes sensuality so intriguing.

"I am naughty!" Emma drawls in a suggestive voice begging for attention.

"We know that." Gracie laughs.

"No, really naughty." Emma's laugh is almost a cackle.

"What do you mean?" Melissa asks, eyes wide.

"Promise not to tell?" Emma lures us into her secret.

"Promise," we say, huddling close.

"I'm sleeping with Peter," she announces and then adds for effect, "and he's totally hot!"

"You vixen!" Raven cries.

"When did all this happen?" Gracie asks.

"Recently." Emma digs her fingers into the M&M bowl. "Remember that night at the dance when he drove me home?"

"Wow, that first night?!" I ask incredulously. *That's just so fast and so wrong!* my radar shouts. They're barely dating. I know he didn't even get her a card for Valentine's. I also know his Facebook profile lists him as single, and that really vexes Em. Now I know why it bothers her so much.

"No!" She elbows me. "Not then. That's when he first kissed me." She shrugs coyly. "Plus a little more."

"This is really . . . big." Melissa paces her words.

"You're being safe, right?" Gracie lays her hand on Emma's arm.

"Whatever." Emma rolls her eyes. "So, anyway, the next night he offered to take me home, and things got hotter and heavier, and he says he's absolutely crazy about me." She bats her thickly mascaraed lashes dramatically. "So not last Saturday, but the one before, after the hockey game."

I flash back to the game.

"Remember, we all hung out for a minute around the locker rooms to congratulate the guys when they came out?"

I nod and pop some M&M's in my mouth to keep from saying anything I'll regret. The sweet chocolate calms me for a second. I feel so anxious for Emma. Why did she do this? And why is she so proud?

"Yeah." Raven leans back against the couch. "Randy and I went home with Mom and Dad, and you're saying something huge happened after we piled into the Explorer."

"Lindsey and Noah had a quick smooch when no one was looking — except me." She glances at me sideways.

I blush. I had hoped no one had seen. I mean, everyone knows Noah and I are together. But, I like the no PDA rule for dance team. It keeps all of our intimate stuff . . . intimate.

"Gracie and Drew hugged, so sweet!" Emma makes kissy lips. "Melissa waited graciously."

"You went home with Peter!" Melissa remembers.

"I did indeed!" Emma shakes her shoulders. "And no one was home at his house. He played this great music, and we did it then and again on Sunday afternoon and Thursday after school, too!"

"Get out!" I'm unable to keep quiet a second longer. "When were you going to tell us?"

"Now." Emma smiles. "I'm telling you now, when I have you all gathered together in one happy place." She raises her eyebrows.

"So, what's it like?" Gracie asks.

"Gracie!" Melissa slaps her.

"Just curious . . ." Gracie shrugs.

"Come on?" Emma raises her eyebrows. "You and Drew never do?"

Gracie shakes her head.

"Did it hurt?" Raven scrunches her nose.

"I thought you were going to wait!" I blurt before Emma can answer. I don't want to accuse her, especially in front of everyone, but I thought that was the deal. I feel like she cheated. I feel like she cheated on me.

It sounds like someone just yanked the cord on my hair dryer — unexpectedly and painfully silent.

"Number one, Miss Perfect . . ." Emma turns to face me. Her voice has morphed from storyteller to litigator. "I never put on a chastity ring or anything. And number two, you're supposed to be my friend, not my mother!"

A total slap in the face! She hates her mom.

"I'm sorry, Em. I'm not saying what you did is wrong. I'm just surprised, that's all." I lean in and hug her. "This is huge and you shocked the daylights out of me." I feel her body shake for one second in my arms. Is she crying or laughing? Then she tightens like a starched shirt.

"Well, you know I love shock value." She pulls back and grins.

CHAPTER FIFTEEN

The sound of skates on the rink is like the sharpening of knives. I shiver as I stand inches from the glass separating me from the ice.

Clack, clack, clack, clack.

The team bangs their hockey sticks against the ice in unison — their way of clapping, Noah explained to me. This signals the end of practice. I stand out of the way as the guys, hulking in their stinky equipment, hop over the wall to the bench, then lumber in their skates to the locker room.

I wait. Boys laugh deep, sporty laughs. Shoulder pads thunder as they fall on the floor and locker doors squeak open and shut. I pull my phone out of my bag and flip through my messages. I think of texting Emma, but don't want to be on the phone when Noah emerges. It's Tuesday, and we've barely seen each other all week. He plays away again this weekend so I'm taking advantage of his rare afternoon practice. I thought we could at least walk home and do homework together.

"Hey, short stuff." Randy ruffles my hair as he walks by with a group of seniors.

"Hey, Randy." I smile.

Peter taps me on the shoulder, turns, and smiles as he exits the glass doors into the lobby with a cluster of players. What Noah said about being a hockey girlfriend has come true. I feel welcome here. No one gives me a hard time, and as far as I know, no one gives him one either.

The rink's empty. And there's Noah, walking out of the locker room with the coach. Slung over his shoulder is his enormous hockey bag. It looks big enough to stash a few dead bodies in it. His other hand rakes his hair wet from the showers. I can't stifle the smile that overtakes my face.

"Right, Coach," he says.

"This weekend, I'm counting on you." The coach whaps him on the back.

Noah nods and walks directly up to me and kisses me on the cheek. "Hey, gorgeous."

"Why is such a pretty girl hanging out with such a ruffian?" The coach laughs.

I peek out from behind Noah and shrug.

"Coach, this is my girlfriend, Lindsey. And don't ask her things like that. She might realize what a mistake she's made."

"Nice to meet you, Lindsey."

"Nice to meet you." I shake his hand.

"See ya, Coach." Noah turns and puts his arm around my shoulder.

"Young love," the coach croons as we walk away.

Noah laughs. "He's just jealous. No way he can get a hottie like you."

"He's probably happily married with a houseful of kids and doesn't care one bit about high school girls." I shake my head.

"He is." Noah stops and turns to me. "So, maybe I'm jealous. I'd like a wife and a houseful of kids."

My heart beats faster than the paparazzi's flashbulbs. "Who do you think could put up with you for the rest of your life?" I ask and keep walking. I smile, without him being able to see my face. I love teasing him and can't wait to hear his response, but I'm not sure I'm brave enough to see his expression.

"I was kind of thinking you might." He catches up to me. "I promise I'll let you watch *The Mighty Ducks* whenever you want, *and* I'll keep our fridge stocked with Gatorade."

"Well, in that case . . ." I giggle. "I'll think about it. But only if I can pick which flavors of Gatorade."

"Deal." Noah shakes my hand.

I know this conversation is all in fun, but beneath the joke is the idea of marriage — of us being married and having kids, together, and Noah is the one who brought it up.

I feel like skipping all the way home, but would rather walk slowly and savor Noah's arm around my shoulder and the electricity when our sides brush.

"So, what are you doing this weekend, while I travel the state in the name of hockey?"

"We're going to the basketball game Friday. I've got halftime and Emma's sleeping over Saturday."

"What about the other girls?" Noah ushers me around a puddle on the sidewalk like a true gentleman.

"I think Drew and Gracie are going out. Melissa's going to visit her cousins, and Raven and her folks are traveling with the team to watch Randy. It's not fair that she gets to see you play."

"You two could trade places. Or, I could kidnap you on our bus, but you'd be bored stiff when I go to the game an hour early and when I'm practicing and watching films and stuff the next day."

"Okay, so the hockey widows will just have to eat popcorn and watch movies without our men." I sigh.

"Widows? Men?" Noah looks confused.

"Emma and me. You and Peter."

Noah's face is blank.

"You know he and Emma are dating."

"I'd hardly call what they're doing dating." Noah laughs. "No offense, Linds, but they're just messing around."

I nod. I feel like I've swallowed nail polish remover, sharp and putrid. Poor Emma! How can Peter do this to her? But isn't she doing it to herself too? I feel sick for both of them.

"You knew that, right?" Noah asks, turning my chin to face him.

"I don't think Emma looks at it like that," I say, the words scraping my throat. I don't want to give her feelings for Peter away, but I thought they were obvious.

"Ohh . . ." Noah nods. "Anyway, we're not them. We're us."

I open my front door, thankful for a way to stop talking about this. "Hi, Mom! Noah and I are here to study."

"You wicked witch!" Kristine's voice bellows from upstairs.

I cringe.

"Don't you talk to me like that, young lady!" Mom shrieks back.

Kristine thunders down the stairs without even glancing in our direction.

The garage door slams behind her.

I hate it when they fight. Kristine is so mean to Mom, yet she really needs help. I wish Mom would run after her and they would hug and cry and work things out. But that never happens. Mom comes to the top of the stairs as if in slow motion and spots us. Clearly she didn't hear us say hello over the volume of the argument.

"Oh, hi." Mom looks defeated. "Sorry you had to see that, Noah. Kristine doesn't agree with my parenting these days."

"No big deal, Mrs. Kraus." Noah smiles.

I swallow a mouthwash of anger and shame and pity. Then Noah's arm is around my back guiding me to the kitchen. He takes my coat off for me and kisses me quickly and softly on the lips, then wraps his arm around me in a safe, warm hug. My shoulders relax and my throat works again.

"Sorry," I eek.

"I'm sorry, Linds." He strokes my cheek. "Sorry you have to go through this. Families are a pain."

"Yeah, especially if they have Kristine in them."

"I'll pray for her and your mom, okay?"

Those words mean more to me than I can express. He'll pray for my family! I wish we were older and could run away and be married right now. But I can't say that to Noah. Instead I whisper, "Thanks."

CHAPTER SIXTEEN

"What's this?!" Dad screams at the top of his lungs.

"What's it look like, Dad?" Kristine's voice is too cool. "It's pot, grass, weed, marijuana. Whatever you want to call it."

"I know what it is!" Dad bellows.

"Then why'd you ask?" Kristine's room is next to mine, so I can hear every word through the thin walls.

"I brought some clean laundry into your room and found this in your drawer." Mom's voice sounds unnaturally shrill.

"How about not snooping in my room?!" Kristine shouts back. "Whatever happened to privacy? I bet you didn't search Miss Priss Lindsey's drawers." Kristine starts laughing like a maniac. She must be stoned. Her cackles shake the wall.

Mom and Dad whisper in the hallway. Something about "tough love" or "leaving it alone," depending on whose voice I strain to hear through Kristine's cackle.

I can't stand it. I walk right past them in the hall. Neither of them look at me or speak to me, like I'm invisible. I hate this empty, longing feeling. I pull my black puffer vest from the mudroom hook and slide on a pair of old Tretorns. I need to escape. The sharp air bites my face. I don't care. I run. At first just down the driveway, then down our street, then my feet run all the way through the neighborhood to Noah's house.

I need Noah right now like a magazine needs a cover girl.

Unlike my parents, he notices me. He cares about me. He loves me. He's there for me. He sees me. I know Kristine is needy. Her personality is fragile and torn, but what about me? Here I am, trying to do things right, to say the right words and to act the right way, but no one notices. Before I know what I'm doing, I'm out of breath and ringing his doorbell.

Noah opens the door. His hair is the messiest I've ever seen it. He's wearing gray sweats and a thick, hooded navy blue sweatshirt. His feet are bare. Even his naked little toes are a comfort to me. He has a curious look on his face. Like why in the world did I show up on his doorstep on a Wednesday night? I dive into his strong, warm frame before he can say anything. I lift my face to look in his eyes and just start kissing him. His lips feel soft and his arms feel warm and strong and safe.

"I missed you," I whisper.

"I missed you too." He murmurs back.

I wanted someone to notice me, and here is Noah enveloping every curve of my body. I'm guessing his parents aren't home because he's kissing me back and sliding his hands up my shirt against my skin, and I want him to. I want him to touch all of me and wrap himself around me until I'm safe in him and can't hear my parents yelling or Kristine's cackle echoing through my brain. He sweeps me off my feet like a fireman and carries me into the den where he gently lays me on the couch. Then he's next to me. I'm nervous, but not for long. Noah is sweet and gentle, and it only hurts for a minute or two. Actually it feels good to feel something, even if it's pain. It reminds me I'm alive. I'm here, even if Mom and Dad don't remember.

When it's all over he kisses me lightly on the lips. A drop of sweat drips from his brow, salty on my tongue. "I love you,

Lindsey," he says. I don't want to move, ever. I just want to stay here with him against me and no one else and no world except us. The ugly uncertain girl I used to be dissolves when I'm with Noah. He makes me feel wanted and beautiful and loved.

"I love you too. I love you so much." I throw my arms around his neck and hold him tight against me. Maybe if I hold on tight enough, he'll never leave.

A door slams and there's a rustling of bags and the clinking of keys. My heart races. My face burns. This is real. It felt like a dream, like a movie I was watching. But it was real. We did this thing and someone is about to find out.

Noah jumps off me and grabs my wadded jeans from the foot of the couch. He tosses them to me and yanks on his boxers and sweats. I feel like I'm four, and my fingers can't get my zipper and snap to work properly. My sweatshirt hits me in the face. I laugh nervously and give up on my snap in lieu of a top. I dive into its fleecy softness and wriggle my arms and head out in record time. Noah sits on the other end of the couch, facing me, and shakes his head vigorously to cue me to something I can't figure out. I face him and he nods again.

"In here, Mom," he calls before Mrs. Hornung even calls for him. My heartbeat booms. I'm sure she can hear it in the kitchen. I fully utilize every second to try to resume the look of a normal person. I smooth my hair and straighten my sweatshirt. I finally force my snap shut.

"Oh, hi guys." She smiles, stuffing her keys into her purse as she peeks into the den. "I didn't know you were coming over, Lindsey?"

My cheeks are hotter than my 370-degree flatiron. I feel like "I had sex with your son!" is written across my forehead in sequins.

"Family trouble," Noah interjects for me.

I've never been more thankful for someone to speak. I haven't even told Noah yet. I nod and dig out some words hidden in the back of my throat. "I'm sorry. I didn't know you weren't home, and I didn't call or anything. Kristine got in trouble—huge trouble—and I didn't want to be around all the yelling. I should have—"

"It's okay, dear." Noah's mom puts her hand on my shoulder. I catch a whiff of outside, still clinging to her clothes. "I'm glad you felt comfortable coming here." Two more pats on my shoulder. "You're always welcome."

"Thank you," I say, peeking at her. Hopefully the guilt in my eyes will pass for the burden of family stress.

"Do you two need a snack or something to drink?"

I look at Noah. We've barely spoken since I got here.

He shakes his head. I follow suit.

"Noah, don't be rude. Make Lindsey something in the kitchen. I just brought back all kinds of good stuff from the grocery: hummus, pretzels, yogurts, you name it."

There's no way I can sit around and snack with Noah and his mom after what just happened. I can't believe this happened! I need to process what we did, or I'm going to implode.

"Thanks, but I really should get going." Noah places his hand on mine. I don't know if he's thanking me for ending this uncomfortable scene or asking me to stay. "My folks don't even know where I am, and they'll worry."

"All right, dear. Hang in there." Mrs. Hornung gives me a completely unexpected hug. Her hug is light and brief. I hug her back.

"Thanks. You're so sweet."

There's a strange tug at my heart. Even though everything seems so right, so perfect with Noah, like true love and fairy tales.

Even though his mom likes me, which means I could have a wonderful mother-in-law. Something's not right, like a puzzle piece is missing. I'd never planned on this.

I walk to the door with Noah holding my hand.

Once in the privacy of the hallway he nuzzles my neck and slides his lips up to my ear where he whispers, "I do love you, Lindsey Kraus. You amaze me."

"And I love you." I look into his eyes, overwhelmed by the intensity I feel for him.

CHAPTER SEVENTEEN

My house is silent. Kristine must have fled the scene of the crime. Mom and Dad must have followed her for once. I open the fridge and grab a Diet Coke. I lean back on the fridge and pop the can. The *sisssle* of escaping carbonation echoes in the empty kitchen. I still smell Noah's minty, boyish scent. I still feel his hair in my fingers. But I can't picture him. These marvelous thoughts keep getting chased away by something, by Someone.

"I know, God. I know I wasn't supposed to. But, this is different. So different. Noah and I love each other." I chase the lump in my throat away with a sip of sweet soda.

The Plain White T's burst into "Hey There Delilah" on my cell phone. I've changed my ring tone to a song from Noah's CD. It's him.

"Hi," I whisper.

"Hi." His voice sounds thick and heavy.

"That was close, huh?"

"Yeah, but I didn't call because of that. I called because I loved being close with you." His voice is so quiet, I squish my ear to the phone to hear him better.

"Me too."

"Are you okay?" Noah asks.

"Yeah," I answer automatically. Am I okay? I hadn't thought

about that. I'm not a virgin anymore. Did it hurt? Was there blood? Will I be condemned? I'm still standing here. I shake my head and the negative thoughts away. "Of course I'm okay. Are you?"

"Never been better."

I listen to his breathing, a soft murmur.

"Gotta run," he whispers. "Love you."

"Love you too."

Snap. I close my phone.

He loves me. He really does love me.

"Lindsey, is that you?"

I swallow, although there's nothing in my mouth. "Yeah, Mom, I'm here." Did I say anything out loud I shouldn't have?

Mom's footsteps are slow and creaky. Her eyes are red and puffy. I should run to her. I should hug her. I should ask if *she's* okay. *Okay.* That's a good question, isn't it? Am I okay? That's exactly what Noah asked me.

"Mom, are you all right?"

She nods. "I just don't know what I'm going to do. Kristine got furious and stormed out of here in Dad's new Audi. He took off in my car to try to find her." A stray tear slides down Mom's cheek. "She could get in an accident."

"Oh, Mom." I reach out and fold my arms around her. "I'm sorry." My heart races. Can she tell Noah was in my arms minutes ago? Do I look different? Am I different?

Mom pats my back and pulls away. "Don't you be sorry. It's Kristine who owes us an apology, but I don't even care about that. I just want her to be safe. She's so reckless. I'm scared for her." Mom sniffles. "I just keep praying." Mom's voice swells.

"I do too." I shake my head.

The garage door groans, and I freeze along with Mom. If it's

Kristine, it will be a scene. If it's Dad, who knows?

"Anne?"

"Lindsey and I are in here."

"Oh, hi, Lindsey." Dad's blond hair is disheveled. His blue eyes seem to have faded to gray, and his ruddy skin is more pink than usual.

"Hi."

"Well?" Mom looks at him expectantly.

"She drove off at a million miles an hour, and I couldn't keep up. I had to stop at the red lights. I drove past that boyfriend's — what's his name's — house and the school and that cheerleader girl, Delaney's. Nothing." Dad exhales.

Mom shakes her head.

I take this as my cue to disappear. They clearly don't need me to hash this out. And in answer to my earlier question, can she tell? The answer is *no*. They don't notice anything is different about me. They don't notice anything about me. I don't think they even want to. No one asked where I was. Did they even notice I was gone? No one asked how all this affects me. Do they even care?

I silently slink to my room, abandoning their strained voices. I flip open my phone and punch in "143" — I love you — and send to Noah.

CHAPTER EIGHTEEN

I sit on the stairs, fiddling with my iPod and waiting for Emma. She's sleeping over tonight, although I wish it were Noah instead. How amazing would it be if we could hold each other all night long? But he has away games tonight and Sunday. The whole team took a bus to a town three hours away, and *their* sleepover is in some random hotel. He'll miss youth group, and I won't see him until Monday at school, and I don't know if I can go that long. I ache when I'm not with him—a weird, lonely, empty feeling.

It's been three days since I had sex. In some ways my life is exactly the same. I go to school. I go to dance rehearsal. I text my friends. I do homework. Kristine is completely wrapped up in herself. Mom and Dad are consumed by Kristine.

In other ways my life has totally changed. I have this enormous secret, but it's not one I want to tell anyone. Who would I tell? My friends? They'd think I'm slutty. Everyone was shocked when Emma told us about her and Peter. Mom? She says she wants me to tell her everything. Who is she kidding? Because of the daily Kristine drama, she doesn't have any time for *me* these days and, even if she did, she would totally flip! Dad? That's funny. He gets home tonight from a sales conference. He's been out of town for the last three days, ever since the Kristine episode. He's not around enough to talk to. Noah? He already knows. That leaves God, and I'm pretty sure I know what He thinks about all of this.

So, it's just me and this secret. This secret that makes me want to dance and laugh because I feel so connected to Noah, like nothing could ever come between us. This secret that at the same time makes me want to run and hide because I know, instinctively, that this isn't how it was supposed to be. Otherwise I could tell my friends and my parents.

Noah and I were supposed to wait. Everything was great between us while we waited. But now, it's so intense. I think about him all the time. I feel displaced when I'm not with him. I count down the minutes until I can see him. I linger at my locker in the mornings, waiting for him to show up and say, "Good morning." I love seeing what he's wearing and how handsome it makes him look. We don't kiss or anything, but he'll whisper something in my ear or brush his fingers against my cheek. Then it's off to class where I force myself to pay attention and pull my pen away from the doodles of "Mrs. Lindsey Hornung" that fill the borders of my notebooks.

During the last five minutes of lunch, Noah and I wander from our tables of friends and find a place to sit alone. We talk with our faces close. He makes me smile and feel like I'm the only thing in his world. I know he's the only thing that matters in mine.

I could tell Emma. She'll be here any minute, and she's not a virgin either. She couldn't judge me. Plus, she's known me forever, and she's a Christian too. So we share the same sin. It sounds so serious when I say *sin*.

Ding-dong.

Emma pushes through the front door without saying a word. Her eyes are bloodshot, and all the freckles on her cheeks have blended into one big splotch.

"Hey, Em," I say. Her neon orange duffle bag with "Emma" monogrammed in silver script letters bumps me as she walks past.

I follow her like the train of an elegant gown. She starts toward the family room.

"Mom's in there," I whisper. Whatever's on Emma's mind, I'm guessing she doesn't want to share with my mom.

She nods and looks at the ceiling. I know she's trying not to cry.

"C'mon." I grab her arm and lead her upstairs.

"Mom!" I yell. "Emma's here. We're going to my room!"

"Okay, sweetie." Mom tries to make her voice sound upbeat, despite the fact Kristine's out with her boyfriend and Mom's worried she won't come home tonight.

I close my door gently.

"What's wrong, Em?" I ask, plopping next to where she's landed on my bed.

"Everything!" she shrieks, finally letting the tears explode. "I missed my period, Linds. No joke." She shakes her head furiously. "I missed my period, which means I might be pregnant!"

I put my arm around her, waiting. I know, after all these years, Emma will need to vent before I can say anything.

"Sixteen and pregnant." She fake grins. "Fabulous. Now I won't have to worry about what I eat—I'll just be fat." She brushes trails of melted mascara from her cheeks with the back of her hand. I stretch over to my dresser and grab a Kleenex. I ease back next to her, handing her the tissue.

"Can you imagine me with a baby?!"

"Have you taken a test? Do you know for sure?" I ask.

"I was too scared to do it alone," she whimpers. "I brought one over. It's in my bag." Emma sniffs. "Will you wait with me?"

"Of course." I'm not sure what she means, but of course. For Em, I'd do almost anything.

We sit a few minutes, holding hands, lost in thoughts. After a while, Emma releases my hand, slides off my bed, and kneels by her bag. She pulls out a white cardboard box and tosses me a folded-up sheet of directions. I read them silently to myself, then shrug.

"Okay, so basically you have to take the plastic cover off the stick, pee on it, and wait for two minutes." I take a deep breath and continue. "It's like in science, there's a control group and an experimental group. One window will have a line to show it's working, the control. The other window will only have a line if you're pregnant, the experiment. One line, not pregnant. Two lines, pregnant." I sound like the commercial.

Emma nods. "Alright." She wipes her tears again with the Kleenex. "Alright, let's do it."

Before I answer, Emma is out the door, down the hall, and in the bathroom. I can't believe Emma might be pregnant. My Emma, who seems like she still needs mothering, could soon be taking care of a teeny, tiny baby. What would she do? What would her parents say? Would she stay in school? Would she and Peter get married? Is she really pregnant? How late is she?

Fwwooooshh! The toilet flushes.

Could *I* be pregnant? Wow! I can't believe I haven't even thought of that. Noah and I only slept together once, but I've heard stories about that happening. What if it was me down the hall? What would I do? Would I tell Noah? Of course. But what would that do to him and hockey scholarships? A daddy at seventeen! And me . . .

Emma stands in my doorway, holding a white stick in her hand the size of a toothbrush. I hate myself for worrying about me. She stares at it, like it's a crystal ball capable of telling the future.

I walk over and slide the stick from her fingers. I place it on my dresser and sit her back on my bed.

"It'll be okay, Em."

"I don't know, Linds."

I glance at the red lights on my digital clock. I search for words of comfort. I'd like to tell Emma that God will be with her. I'd like to know He'll be with me. But will He? When we've broken the rules? Doesn't God punish people who disobey? I swallow a lump in my throat the size of a hockey puck.

"How late?" I choke.

"*Eight* days," Emma whispers.

"Why didn't you tell me?" I ask. Inside I wonder if I were late, would I tell Emma? I haven't even told her what I've done.

"Oh, please." Emma gestures. "You've been so wrapped up in Mr. Messyhair that you wouldn't have heard me anyway."

"Ouch!" Can't she see I'm in love? Can't she see I have stuff going on too? I scrunch my lips. Doesn't anybody except Noah see what's going on with me?

"It's true, Linds." Emma turns to face me. "Every day at lunch, you're so smitten, it's sick."

"I love him," I whisper. Now it's my turn for tears.

"Get out!" Emma's eyes expand. "Who said it first?"

"Noah." I shrug and smile. I can tell she cares a little.

"Wow. That's serious! I guess I've been pretty consumed too." Emma rolls her eyes in that mischievous way she has. "I forgive you for being a selfish friend, if you forgive me for being a selfish friend."

"Deal." I smile and reach out my hand. We shake hands with mock formality and then hug.

"Em," I begin, "what will Peter say?"

Her body shakes in my arms. "Who knows? He never says much of anything."

I glance back at my clock. "It's time." I give her an extra squeeze. "Do you want to look, or do you want me to?"

CHAPTER NINETEEN

On Sunday morning I wake up first. It's almost noon! Emma and I were up late celebrating the results of her pregnancy test — negative! — over enormous ice-cream sundaes.

In those minutes of not knowing, I saw Emma's whole life turn into chaos, like Job's in the Bible. Then I pictured mine doing the same thing. After all, I could just as easily be pregnant. Sure, Noah and I are in love, which does not appear to be the case for Peter and Emma, but we've all had sex, and Noah and I did not use a condom. So, does that make my act any different from hers? Yesterday morning I would have said what Noah and I did was different, but the outcome could be exactly the same. I don't know anymore.

I can't imagine how relieved Emma is. I don't want to wake her. I'm sure she's exhausted from carrying around all that anxiety.

The alluring aroma of sausage fills my nostrils. I give in to daylight and quietly crawl out of my covers. I rub my eyes on the way downstairs.

"Good morning, sunshine." Dad beams from the stove.

"Hi, Dad."

"I thought you girls would be hungry." He flips a pancake high in the air, does a spin, and catches the flapjack in his skillet. "Where's Emma?"

"Still sleeping. She didn't know there was a show going on down here." I smile. It's nice having Dad home. He really is great, as far as dads go. He's just gone so much! I miss him.

"Well, sit down, princess." He motions toward the stools at the island in front of him. "Because the old pops has prepared a feast."

"So I see," I say, pretend curtsying. "Where are Mom and Kristine?"

Dad's face tightens. "Your sister is a no-show. Mom is changing out of her church clothes." He manages a strained grin. "We missed you this morning. Pastor John had some good stuff."

A pang of guilt stabs my heart. I slept right through church. Well, I did have a sleepover. Still. What would God have said to me this morning? Would He have been happy to see me?

"You could have woken me up," I mumble.

"We didn't have the heart." Dad places a steaming plate of pancakes and sausage in front of me.

"Thanks." I don't know if I'm thanking him for the food or the reprieve from church.

The pancakes are sweet and fluffy and melt in my mouth. "Dad, your pancakes are the absolute best!"

"If they're the best, then I want some." Emma plops onto the stool next to me. "G'morning, Mr. Kraus."

"Good morning, Emma. It's been too long since I've seen you!" He ladles more batter into his pan. "What's new?"

Emma and I look at each other and out of nervousness start giggling. If only he knew! We laugh so hard, we can't stop.

/ / /

Emma stays the day. We give ourselves manicures and bake a double batch of peanut butter bars—something we've been doing since fifth grade. Somehow all that gooey peanut butter and sweet dough calms our nerves and makes life simple again. After stuffing our faces with warm goodies and about a half gallon of cold milk, we head to the mall for some therapeutic shopping.

"Thanks, Dad," I say as he drops us at the main entrance. "Are you up for a checkers tournament tonight?"

"Sorry, sweetie. I have to write a report and pack. I'm headed out again tomorrow — St. Louis, this time."

Emma's waiting on the sidewalk. There's another car behind us.

"I wish you didn't have to go on another trip," I pout.

He cradles my chin in his hand. "Sweetheart, if Daddy didn't travel for work, you couldn't buy all those fabulous clothes. Someone has to pay the Visa bill." He winks and waves. "Have fun. I'll pick you up at six. We'll play checkers when I get back." He pulls the door shut and drives away.

I don't get the chance to tell him that I'd rather have him home than reap the rewards of his fat paycheck. Don't get me wrong. I *love* to shop! I take great pleasure in a pair of perfect-fitting jeans. But I miss my daddy! And so does Mom. I know she does. And, Kristine? Well, clearly Kristine missed him somewhere along the way. I don't know if she does what she does to get his attention or to get attention from someone else since he's never home. But I know *I* feel hollow knowing he's leaving again.

In the shoe department of Nordstrom Emma asks, "So, what do you think about youth group tonight?" She doesn't look at me, but keeps her eyes glued to a patent flat she's holding. I realize if we're going to make it, we'll need Dad to take us straight from the mall to church.

I don't want to be the one to say we shouldn't go. I mean we already missed church this morning, but I'm not really in the mood. I'll go if Emma wants to. I'll leave it up to her.

"Whatever," I say, roaming to the next rounder of shoes.

"I don't know." Emma looks at the price on the bottom of some fringed boots. "I just don't feel like it's right to go tonight, with everything going on and stuff."

"No big deal." I nod, secretly relieved. "We'll go next week."

"Yeah, we'll go next week," Emma says, biting her lip. "Plus, the boys won't be back tonight anyway. Who would we flirt with?" She winks.

CHAPTER TWENTY

"What time do you have practice today?" Noah asks as the bell signals the end of lunch.

"Not until four. There's something going on in the church gym at our normal time. I have dead time between school and practice. I guess I'll plow through some homework right after school so I'm not up all night studying."

Noah gazes into my eyes with a dreamy look.

"What's going on in there?" I ask.

"I *thought* you said something about later practice when we were on the phone last night. My practice was this morning, so I'm free and clear." He nods and leans close. "I've just been trying to figure out how to get you alone again."

I know my face is as crimson as my Roses Are Red nail polish. Crowds of students shuffle on their way to class.

"Can I drive you home after school?"

"Sure." I smile, not daring to look at him. I'm not supposed to ride in a car with boys, but Mom will be at work, and that's the least of my worries! I've thought a lot about if we'll do it again. I mean, I guess once you've slept together, you continue to sleep together. And it's made Noah and me so close. We have this amazing secret that no one knows about. *Well, okay, God, You know about it, but You're not who I want to talk to about all of this. Sorry,*

I just don't think You understand what it's like. And, I do love him. I feel wiggly all over.

"Do you think anyone will be home?" Noah asks.

I'm walking toward my locker, and he's following. "Don't know." I shrug, still too embarrassed to look at him.

"I'll meet you here, okay?" Noah grabs my hand and gives it a squeeze. He's giving me room to get out of this if I want.

"Okay." I squeeze back. "See ya."

My last three classes are awful. I can't concentrate at all. In my head, I play back Noah and I having sex. Meanwhile the youth group lesson about getting burned plays like an overtrack in my mind. Even a picture of Adam and Eve flashes through my brain! I picture Emma's pregnancy test. I think of that chastity rally. But, I always come back to how soft Noah's lips are and how gentle his hands feel on my back. He makes me feel beautiful.

/ / /

When the last bell rings, I don't know if I'm relieved or terrified.

"Hockey season's winding down for the year, and then we can be together every weekend, Linds." The windshield wipers creak, brushing fat raindrops off his windshield.

"Yay!" I smile. "I missed you last weekend. It's weird when you're gone."

"Just two more weeks. Then I'm yours." Noah stops at a traffic light, leans over and kisses me, right in the middle of town. I close my eyes and inhale his breath and savor his lips on mine. I want to marry this boy!

I unlock the front door.

"Mom!" I call out. "Kristine?"

Silence. The lights are out in the hallway and kitchen. Noah looks around and tiptoes behind me. I'm not supposed to have boys over when my parents aren't home, and I suppose this is why.

"I know Dad's on another trip and won't be home until late tomorrow. Looks like we have the house to ourselves."

The air is heavy with my words. Noah and I have barely shared a quick kiss since our romantic interlude a week ago.

"So," I say to fill the pause.

"So," Noah whispers, turning me to him. He leans over, and he's kissing me and he wraps his arms around my back, and I feel warm all over, and I can barely breathe. I forget where I am and what I'm wearing and that we're breaking all the rules. Noah's hands slide under my shirt, and they're tugging at my bra, and I don't push him away. He unbuttons my jeans, then his. He walks and guides me, kissing me the whole time, to the family room, where he lowers me onto the couch. He pushes our pants around our ankles and his mouth is on mine and his hands are touching every part of me. I'm hot and dizzy.

"Lindsey." Mom's voice breaks through my dream state, like glass shattering, from somewhere upstairs.

I push Noah away while rehooking my bra. "Yeah, Mom, I just got home." I exhale to steady myself and inhale to try to catch more air. "Noah drove me home." I tug up my jeans. Did my voice crack?

Noah pulls up his jeans, ruffles his hair, and pushes up the sleeves on his barn jacket, which he's still wearing. His cheeks look like I've rubbed them with blush.

Mom treads down the stairs, and again I wonder if she knows. Does she know what she's interrupted? Does she know Noah and I were having sex? Again?

"I thought you had practice. Hi, Noah." She looks around the house. "It's dark down here."

Noah shoves his hands in his pockets. "Hi, Mrs. Kraus."

"Yeah," I defend myself. "We don't practice until four, and it was raining, so Noah gave me a ride. We just got here, and I called for you, you must not have heard me, and we didn't even get a chance to turn the lights on. It is dark in here when it's cloudy." All of this is true, I tell myself.

"My last appointment canceled today, so I decided to come home early and tackle my closet. I can't hear anything with my head buried in there." She looks us up and down as if she's on to us.

Mom takes the lead toward the kitchen. "You two need a snack?" She flicks on the fluorescent lights.

"Sure, Mom." I say. My voice sounds metallic bouncing off the empty wall.

"Sounds great, Mrs. Kraus." Noah's voice sounds strange too.

"Help yourselves. I just came down to get a marker to label some of those crates in my closet." Mom rummages through her desk drawer and disappears back down the hall with a Sharpie. She turns.

"When's practice?" she asks.

"Four." I answer.

"I can take you, if you want. Just let me know when you're ready." Her voice fades as she climbs the stairs.

Noah's eyes are glued on me with the look of a ravenous tiger. "I want you," he mouths silently.

I shake my head.

Mom's footsteps echo up the stairs and toward her room.

He leans forward and kisses me again. His lips are hot, and although I ache to be near him, this is going nowhere with Mom just a flight of stairs away. I use all of my inner strength to step back.

I shake my head. "No fair," I whisper.

"Definitely not fair," he whispers back. His fingers weave through his dark locks. "Saturday," he says.

"Saturday?" I ask.

"Saturday." He nods. "I have a Friday night game and a day game Saturday, but that leaves Saturday night. Randy and Raven are having a luau. We'll leave early. If my parents go out, we could stop by my house." He sounds out of breath. "I need to be with you."

Noah is usually so cool and in control. I'm agitated seeing him desperate like this. But I also feel more in love with him. He wants me that much!

I kiss him quickly on the mouth. "I love you."

"I love you too." He wraps his arms around me. I close my eyes and bury my face in him.

"See ya tomorrow."

I nod.

"Bye, Linds." He bites his lower lip and opens the door.

"Bye." I watch him walk down my driveway and exhale. My head and heart are too full. I should sit and sort through all of these emotions. I should pray about it or something, but I can't. It's too much. It's too over the top. I flip open my phone and punch in Raven.

PLAN 4 WKEND?

I text.

CHAPTER TWENTY-ONE

Saturday afternoon Raven and I went to the home hockey game. We wore Randy's and Noah's away jerseys. As Melissa said, "There's only so much hockey you can *stick* us with, Lindsey."

After the game I scurry to get ready for the luau at the Macks'. I put on a truly obnoxious floral tank top with a pair of my favorite jeans and flip-flops. I slide a grass skirt over my jeans. I find a plastic flower from Mom's craft cupboard and tuck it behind my right ear. My sunglasses complete the look. "Crazy," I mumble to myself as I look in the bathroom mirror.

"What's the occasion?" Kristine's mellow voice rolls into the bathroom. "Trick or treat early this year?"

She looks horrible. Her eyes are pink and squinty. She hasn't washed her hair in days.

"Raven's having a luau." I slide my sunglasses down my nose and wink. "Want to come?"

"Not." Kristine disappears into the cave of her bedroom.

I twirl in front of the mirror and watch the strands of plasticine grass swoosh out around me.

"Did Kristine come this way?" Mom sounds exhausted.

"In her room." I motion.

"Thanks." Mom continues down the hall. She doesn't even notice I'm dressed like a hula dancer or wearing flip-flops.

"Hey there, Delilah, what's it like in New York City?" my phone sings.

"Yeah?" I answer.

"We're pulling into your driveway." Emma's laughing.

I click my phone shut and slick on more lip gloss.

"Bye, Mom!" I shout as I race down the steps.

"Where are you going?" Her head peaks around the railing.

"Raven's. Remember, she's having a luau? Gracie's driving?" I told Mom all of this earlier in the week. *She* took me to the dollar store to get the grass skirt yesterday. Is she *that* tuned-out to me?

"Oh, right. Sorry, sweetie." Mom sounds genuinely sorry. "Have fun. Be home by midnight, okay?"

"Okay, bye." I slam the front door behind me. What would she do if I said no or if I just didn't bother coming home? Kristine does it all the time. It's a relief to be free of the ever-present pressure filling the walls of our house. I breathe deeply, then dash to Gracie's car.

"Cool do, Mel!" I squeal. Melissa's hair is in dozens of skinny braids. She's wearing a jean skirt and a big Hawaiian shirt. Emma has on a neon lime green miniskirt with a tight white tank and a floral shirt unbuttoned like a jacket over it. Gracie wears red capris and a navy-and-white-striped nautical top with red espadrilles.

When we get to the Macks', Raven drapes colorful silk leis around our necks. Randy has a reggae mix jamming. Mr. Mack stands outside wearing a hat and mittens and grilling kabobs. Randy, Noah, and some other hockey players loiter around the grill.

"Who all wants a piña colada?" Mrs. Mack drawls as we make our way into the kitchen. We stare at her and the pitcher of white creamy drink she's holding. I wonder if my friends are thinking what I'm thinking.

"They're virgin." Raven laughs. "No alcohol, y'all!"

Virgin. The word slaps me in the face.

Everyone takes a frothy cup. Mine chills the inside of my sweaty hand.

"To best friends!" Gracie says, raising her glass. We all clink cups and sip sweet fruitiness.

"To Mrs. Mack!" Emma yells. "These things are awesome!"

I look out the window again. Did Noah even notice I'm here?

Ding-dong.

Raven skitters to the door with another lei.

It's Peter. I recognize his voice. So does Emma. I see her glance toward the entryway.

"Where's Drew tonight?" I ask Gracie, trying to draw Emma's attention away from the door.

"He had some family thing." She fake pouts.

Peter walks right past us to the porch without a glance at Emma.

"Why don't we go outside and see what the boys are doing?" Emma asks.

"How about, instead, we make fun of the boys by watching them through the window?" Raven saves Emma, and maybe me, too, from looking like lovesick puppies. She positions herself in a chair by the window, opens the blinds, grabs the candlestick sitting on the table, and using it as a microphone, announces, "Funnier than a sitcom, cuter than the guys on *Grey's Anatomy*, all here on my very own porch, I'm pleased to unveil our season premiere of *The Hockey Hunks.*"

We all sit and take turns narrating.

"Gee, guys, aren't we big and strong?" Gracie says in a deep voice, passing the candle to Emma.

"Do you think anyone exists in the world except for us?" Emma bellows.

"Probably not." Melissa sighs, twirling a piece of pineapple on a toothpick. "I mean, the world is the ice rink, right?"

After a while the boys carry in trays of teriyaki chicken and skewered veggies.

"Hey, gorgeous." Noah leans in and tucks my hair behind my ear. "Extremely exotic." He taps my plastic flower. "How do you expect us natives to behave ourselves?"

I can't believe I worried if he noticed me. After everything we've done, I'm still so insecure. It's stupid.

I eat until I feel like I'm going to bust. Mr. and Mrs. Mack hold a limbo stick. We take turns going under until it's so low I have to practically do a backbend. I tumble to the floor. Randy and Raven keep at it until everyone else is out.

"You two must have been practicing all week!" Tyler, a skinny guy with thick glasses, accuses.

Noah grabs me by the arm and whisks me outside while Randy and Raven take bows.

"At last, alone," he whispers. He's kissing me soft and slow. His back is to the window, so I'm kind of hidden behind his height. I tingle all over and feel dizzy, like I'll stop breathing if I stop kissing him.

"How are we going to get alone?" he whispers between kisses.

I keep kissing him. I can't think about being alone with him. Things will definitely get out of hand—again. But, I can't *not* think about it either. My body pulls toward him like a magnet to metal. I want him to touch me.

"Your house?" I gasp.

"Dad has a sore throat. They canceled their plans." Noah shakes his head and traces his fingers down my spine.

The hollow echo of fist on glass makes me jump. Randy is at the window pounding and making kissy faces. Like the knock shattered the silence, Randy's expression dissolves our steamy reverie. I laugh so hard, it almost quiets the voices tugging at my heart and body. Looks like sex will wait, which is oddly freeing. I never knew sex would be such an ominous cloud, lurking in the sky like a storm ready to strike. The anticipation is unbearable.

We eat gooey mango tarts for dessert, and Mrs. Mack teaches us how to hula. Before I know it, it's 11:40.

"Hey, Gracie, I'm supposed to be home at midnight." I shrug toward the clock.

"Me, too!" Melissa screams, then puts her hand over her mouth. "Oh my gosh, I can't be late. My folks will kill me. I know they'll be waiting up for me." She grabs her coat and thanks Mr. and Mrs. Mack for the party.

"Alright, girls. Let's not turn into pumpkins." Gracie pulls her car keys out of her purse.

I kiss Noah lightly on the lips. "Good night."

"Not quite the night I envisioned," he whispers for only me to hear.

I lean back and shrug.

We all thank the Macks and hug Raven and gather our things — everyone but Emma, who's lounging in a beanbag.

"You coming?" I ask.

"Curfew, schmurfew." She laughs. "I think I'll hang out for a bit."

"How are you getting home?" Melissa asks innocently.

Emma rolls her eyes and tilts her head toward Peter, who I haven't even seen her talk to all night.

I usher Melissa out the front door before she lets her next words escape.

"She's not —" She starts on the front step.

I cup my hand over her mouth. "Looks like it," I whisper.

"What do you guys think about that?" Gracie, asks unlocking the car.

"I don't know what to think," Melissa confesses. "It's way over my head."

"I know she's getting hurt, but it's almost like she wants to," I add. "I just wish Peter was nicer to her."

"I just wish she had more respect for herself," Gracie says calmly, not accusingly. "Emma's so great. She doesn't have to act like this."

No one said the word *sex*. But we all thought it.

CHAPTER TWENTY-TWO

Something about wearing black always makes me feel put together, sleek. I'm wearing a black V-neck cashmere sweater with a tight white tee positioned perfectly underneath. My black studded belt looped through my jeans looks fab with these boots. Noah will have a hard time focusing on Pastor Ed at youth group.

"Thanks, Mom," I say as she pulls up to the door of the Youth Barn.

"Sure, honey. I'll pick you girls up later." Mom smiles and waves. She's driving both ways tonight.

"Thanks, Mrs. Kraus," Emma calls as she crawls out behind me.

I feel anxious after not being at youth group last week. I mean, no one takes attendance or anything, but still Emma and I made a conscious decision to skip. I let Emma open the door, and I pause before stepping inside. The drummer is practicing a cadence, and the air is charged. Kids swarm the snack station and gather in small groups, giggling and slapping high fives. I feel like a voyeur, watching a scene where I don't belong. I glance from side to side, anxious to find something. What am I searching for?

"C'mon," Emma says, grabbing my arm.

I follow, breathing in the smell of new carpet and gym shoes.

"Ladies . . ." Peter stands to make room for us on a pile of pillows near the stage.

Emma playfully punches his shoulder. I'm glad they're getting along tonight.

I feel a magnetic pull toward Noah. Like he was the thing I was hoping to find, and now I've found it.

"Hey." I smile. He snuggles me next to him. His arm feels so natural around my shoulders, like I belong here. I bop my head to the drumbeat. The energy is contagious. There's electricity in this room.

"Howdy, ladies and gents!" Pastor Ed jumps on stage. He's wearing a plaid shirt and a hokey bandana tied around his neck. "First a few announcements, and then we'll get on with the show."

"Show?" I whisper to Noah.

He shrugs.

I look to Emma. She's studying Peter, who's eyeing the tall brunette sitting catty-corner in front of him.

"As a follow-up to our heated discussion . . ." Pastor Ed pauses while the drummer gives a *ba dum dum*. "Thank you." Pastor Ed nods. "As I was saying, to follow up our heated discussion on *s-e-x*, I want to announce a rally coming to town in two weeks called The Silver Ring Thing. They'll have rockin' music, awesome prayer, and everyone attending receives a Bible plus a chastity ring."

Noah holds my hand tightly, like he's willing me to be calm. Like his hand is saying, "It's okay, Linds. We love each other."

Emma sniggers and tosses her head.

I pull my hand away and trace my ring finger with my thumb. I don't want to be a conspirator on this. I don't want to hide something from God. I feel nervous again, like I need to find something I've lost. What have I lost?

Oh, God, what have I done? I press my lips together tighter than an eyelash curler clamping.

A month ago I would have urged Emma to come with me to the rally, especially if it had great tunes. Now neither of us can go. We've lost the right. What I've lost is my virginity! My stomach churns and lilts. And I can't get it back—ever! Beads of sweat break out on my hairline. My cheeks and eye sockets tingle. I feel dirty all over, soiled. This isn't Emma's fault or Noah's fault. It's all mine, and I have to live with the consequences forever. This is something I can't undo. It's not like yelling at my sister, then saying I'm sorry and trying not to get angry with her again. It's not like anything. I was a virgin, and now I'm not! The lump in my throat feels like I've swallowed the chastity ring I'll never be able to wear. There's a pinching in the top of my nose. I try to shake it away, but the tears are coming. They're pooling in the corners of my eyes. I've got to get out of here. I stand and race toward the restrooms.

"Linds, you okay?" I hear Noah whisper.

But I keep walking, ignoring him, my back to Noah and the crowd. I can't look at him. I love him. No, I hate him. No, I hate what we did! Everything blurs as tears pour down my face like hot water from a shower. Pastor Ed's voice fades into a monotone blip, like the grown-ups on Charlie Brown. *Waa. Wa. Wa. Waap.*

The path from my seat to the bathroom feels like a mile-long trek. I walk and I walk and I walk like I'm on a treadmill until I'm finally behind the safety of the closed door. A sob escapes my throat, thick and heavy. I lock myself in a stall. My head collapses on the cold, metal door. Tears pour out for each of the thoughts I've stifled over the past two weeks.

- I love Noah. I love him so much. This alone could bring on tears.

- He loves me too. I truly believe that.
- We had sex. We did, and I actually liked it. I wanted to be with him — to be that connected. Everything I've ever learned says that makes me naughty. That's hard to think out loud. I liked something that was taboo. Sounds like the Garden of Eden and that blasted apple. God never said sin wouldn't be fun. He just says we shouldn't do it, so we don't get hurt — hurt by things and ideas sometimes we can't even understand.
- It was wrong. We knew we shouldn't do it. Scratch that, I knew I shouldn't do it, and I did it anyway. I can't hold Noah accountable. I think in my head I've been saying, "Well, he's a Christian too, and he thought it was okay." That's between him and God, not him and me. We barely talked about our views on sex as Christians before we did it. I mean, that time after the dance was just like joking. I should have asked Noah what he thought. I should have prayed about it. I knew having sex with Noah was wrong all along, but I didn't want to listen to God.

I grab a wad of toilet paper and mop some of the soppy mess of tears and makeup from my face. It's a relief to let these thoughts surface instead of pushing them away and hiding them in the back of my mind. My thoughts have been there, I just wouldn't allow myself to see them. The something I was looking for when I walked in tonight wasn't Noah. It was Jesus.

My tears slow to a trickle. The salty tracks they've left on my face are beginning to sting. I inhale and exhale. I'm going to have to go back out there. I don't think I can. How am I going to do this?

God? My instinct tells me to turn to Him, like anytime I need strength or courage. But I've been ignoring this sixth sense lately. I can't imagine He wants to hear from me. I've completely turned my back on Him. Where else can I turn? I hope He's still there. *Oh, God, please still be there!*

God? I pray. *I'm sorry. I'm so sorry. I've made an enormous mistake. I really do love Noah.* I exhale and think of Noah's eyes and his soft hands, and I have to shake my head to get back to God. I pray out loud to push away the thoughts that have been keeping me from Him. *I should have waited. I knew that before, and I know it now. I don't know what happened. I know I've disappointed You. I don't know what I'm going to do next or how I'm going to do it.* My voice cracks as I choke on more tears.

Do I have to break up with Noah? I don't want to! What if I just don't sleep with him anymore? Will he still want to date me if those are the rules? I think he'll understand. Maybe he won't. What will I do then? I look up at the ceiling tiles, as if looking toward heaven will give me the answer I want. I stop shaking and am able to catch my breath.

Slow down, a Voice tells me. *One step at a time.* I don't know if it's me, or God telling me that, but I look down and back up again.

Anyway, Jesus, I can't swallow all of that. Not yet. It's too much! But I do know I need to walk out there and, and what? What is it I need to do? The words come instantly and effortlessly to my heart and my lips: *And listen to the message and sing praises and pray. The rest will fall into place.*

An overwhelming sense of calm rolls through me, like when they wrap that steaming towel around my face during a facial. Everything around me is blocked out, and all I feel is warmth and comfort. My shoulders roll back. I stand up straight and wipe my eyes. I can do this. I can walk back out there and not care what anyone thinks about me bolting to the bathroom. Probably no one noticed, except Emma and Noah, and I'll have to explain to both of them anyway. The explaining will be hard, but walking out there won't. *God will take care of my tomorrow too.* Yes, I'm supposed to live one day at a time, according to Matthew 6:34. I smile at the way Scripture enters my head freely when I'm talking with God again.

I emerge from my hiding place and splash cold water on my face at the sink. I reapply lip gloss and mascara and am thankful the lighting is horrible out there. It might help camouflage my puffy eyes.

The band is jamming. The crowd claps and sings, "Open the eyes of my heart. I want to see You."

My feet walk with the rhythm, and my head bobs to the band. A small laugh escapes my lips. *Thanks for the eye-opener.* I smile at God. He doesn't miss a beat.

I slide into my spot next to Noah. He turns to me with his eyebrows bunched up in concern. I just nod and smile and keep singing. The tunes are a perfect guise to avoid explaining—for now.

Ed has allowed for absolutely no downtime tonight, which is perfect. We go from the songs to Ed's sermon to some silly scavenger hunt around the barn. When it's time to go, Mom's Prius is first in line for pickups. Noah squeezes my hands and searches my eyes. He knows something's wrong.

"I love you," he whispers in my ear as Emma and I start toward Mom's car.

"Me too." I force a smile.

My bottom has barely touched the cool leather in the backseat when my phone buzzes.

R U OK?

"Geez!" Emma rolls her eyes. "One minute without his princess and he's already texting! That's sick!"

Mom laughs. "Have fun, girls?"

I'm typing back.

K. NEED 2 TALK 2U

"Yeah, it was good, right, Linds?" Emma elbows me.

"Yeah. We did this scavenger thingy. Em's team won."

CYT

GR8 143

I type back. I don't want him to think I'm mad at him, because I'm not. My "me too" on the way out was lame, but I'm not sure how I feel right now. I don't know what I'm going to say.

God, I'll need Your help.

In the silence I sense a Voice saying, *I'm always here.*

CHAPTER TWENTY-THREE

My stomach flips, then flops. My brain can't focus, and I'm even struggling to pull an outfit together this morning. I settle for plain jeans and a long-sleeved solid hot pink sweater. A pink polka-dot headband makes me look peppier than I feel. I eat maybe two bites of cereal.

At lunch, I try to listen to Emma lament about how her little brother's Tinker Toys have overtaken her room and about the new songs Raven downloaded last night and about the funny book Melissa's reading and about the fight Gracie and her brother got in this morning over hogging the bathroom. But I keep glancing at the clock, counting the minutes until Noah appears.

"Hey, Linds." Noah's voice sounds mechanical behind me. I turn and force a half smile. He tilts his head toward a small empty table. I nod and scoot out of my chair.

"See ya.'" I wave to my friends and raise my eyebrows. None of them have a clue what I've done, or what I'm about to do.

Dear God, please help me through this. I know it's all my fault, but I need You so much.

"So, are you okay?" Noah asks as we sit down.

I scrunch my nose to push back the tears.

"Hey," he whispers and gently cradles both of my hands in his warm, strong ones. "Are you okay? Are we okay?" His voice quivers.

I nod so many times, I feel like a bobble head. I inhale and look down at our fingers. "It's the chastity ring thing." My words come out, but each one feels like it has to climb over a bump to escape my mouth.

Noah nods and keeps rubbing my fingers, waiting for me to say more.

"I always thought I'd get one, and now—" My voice breaks.

"You don't need one." Noah's lips curve into a half grin. "Wow, Linds, I thought you were going to break up with me." He lets go and leans way back in his chair. My Noah is back—the relaxed, in-control Noah.

My words come more freely, since he's at ease. "I can't have one." I shake my head. "Can't you see, we shouldn't have . . . you know, we should have waited."

"Waited for what? For marriage?"

I nod.

"Linds, we don't need that. You know I love you, and if I haven't told you . . ." Noah leans forward so close his nose almost touches mine. "I'm going to marry you. I want that with you. I want a house and kids and everything."

I feel like I've had an extreme makeover! Before picture: I'm nervous, anxious, and scared Noah will never want to speak to me again. After picture: I'm relieved, elated, excited. My whole future, with Noah, is ahead of me. I feel my heart pounding inside my chest like stilettos on pavement.

"You do?" I eek. A tear escapes my right eye and darts down my cheek. I wipe it, laughing, with the backside of my hand.

"Yeah." There are tears in the corners of Noah's mossy eyes too, confirming his love, melting my concerns.

All other thoughts fly from my head. Noah wants to marry me! *That's different, God, right?* I don't wait for God's reply. This is too good to be true!

"Me too."

"So, we're good. I mean, we're great!" He laughs thick and full, like his laugh came from all those hockey pads he wears. "I mean, I know the Bible says that we're supposed to wait, but in the Bible all those people got married when they were like thirteen or something! We're older than that already, and we're going to get married. We both want that." He gives a cockeyed grin. "We both want that," he whispers.

I nod. I want that too. It feels like that's all I want.

"Making love with you just makes me feel closer to you." Noah squeezes my hands.

Brrriinnng!

Chairs squeak across the floor, shoes pound the ground, books slam, and trash whooshes into garbage cans. Hundreds of conversations buzz around us.

"I can't get another tardy in calculus." Noah grins. "Call me after practice this afternoon?" He leans in to kiss me.

I instinctively take a step back, smile, and shake my finger.

"Yeah, yeah, yeah, no PDA! Whatever!" He turns.

"I love you." I blow him a kiss.

"Me too, Mrs. Hornung." Noah winks and disappears in the crowd.

Mrs. Hornung? Wow, he really wants to marry me!

CHAPTER TWENTY-FOUR

All week I'm bombarded with sex. My new issue of *Lucky* calls for new subscribers with, "Feeling Lucky?" Beer commercials, sitcoms, even the novel I'm reading for English, *Rebecca*, are full of torrid sex. All these allusions to sex make me feel as queasy as if I've woken up to a face covered with oozing zits!

I try to convince myself what Noah said is true. The Bible was written for people two thousand years ago, but that's not what I've grown up believing. I've been taught the Bible is God's Word — His living word. My new pastor, my old pastor, and even Ed at youth group talk about the Bible as the Christian handbook. Jesus ascended into heaven and left His words for us to live by.

I'm glad I talked to Noah. I mean, at least I told him I'd hoped for a chastity ring. But, I'm still unsettled. He does this thing to me. I feel all straight with God, and then Noah is so dreamy, it's hard to stay focused on what God and I talked about. What Noah said about getting married turned our talk a one-eighty and added a whole new dimension to our relationship. We're whispering about weddings at lunch. We're giggling about names for children and what our house will look like when we study together. I feel even closer to him than when we first slept together. Now we have another secret to share.

But I feel like two separate people. I didn't resolve the sex thing. I left the cafeteria Monday feeling fabulous, but afterward I realized Noah thinks sex is okay because we love each other. Still, I know in my heart God doesn't want me to do this. We haven't been alone again. Noah was out of town for hockey all weekend, so I didn't have to face it, but the whole idea of sex eats at me. I don't know if I have enough courage to have another sex talk with Noah.

When I look in the mirror, I see a girl who's not a virgin. I think I was prettier before. I had a more innocent look. Now I feel I have a hardness, an edge — the edge Kristine and her crowd wear like a badge of honor, only I don't feel so proud.

I still need to come clean with this sin.

/ / /

On Sunday Mom, Dad, and I go to church.

Pastor John is small, probably only five foot seven. He's round and bearded like a jolly dwarf. Despite his small stature, his voice fills the sanctuary, and his words carry more weight than Mr. America can lift.

He reads the gospel about the woman at the well. I've heard it so many times my mind drifts. I remember back to a Sunday school lesson. We took turns pulling up a bucket from a plastic toy wishing well. On each kid's pull, the bucket held a piece of candy and a Bible verse. My mind drifts to Noah, and I silently pray he'll play his best in his game today. I wonder if he'll be home in time for youth group.

"Let me tell you a little bit about what was going on here." Pastor John's booming voice breaks my reverie. "The woman came at noon. Everyone else would have come in the morning to avoid the heat. This woman doesn't want to be seen, but who's there?" He stuffs his hands in his pockets. "Jesus." He pauses for emphasis. "Sound familiar?"[2] He paces around the front of the room, back and forth, letting this sink into our ears and hearts. "Is there anything you don't want anyone to know about? Anything you don't want someone to see about you? Well, Jesus knows about it."

My chest burns as if the scarlet *A* has been branded on to my flesh. I want to cover my ears like I did when I was little and heard an ambulance wailing past. If I can't hear Pastor John, maybe I won't have to face what he's saying. It's like I'm watching a horror film. I want to look away, yet I'm riveted to the screen. Despite my shame and fear, I need to hear what's next.

"Remember, He told the woman everything she ever did. So imagine if tonight you're watching TV, and in walks Jesus. He looks you in the eyes and tells you everything you ever did." Pastor John rolls back on his heels. "Would you be okay with that?" There's a long uncomfortable pause. I don't think I'm the only person squirming in my seat.

"But here's the thing. Did He judge the woman? Did He pick up a rock and start stoning her, as was the custom in the day? Did He spit on her or even walk away?" Pastor John shakes his head. "He asks her for a drink of water."

I bite my tongue. That's not too bad, but what does that mean for me?

"You see, Jesus knows everything we do, every secret in the darkest corners of our hearts and *He loves us anyway!*" Pastor John's voice crescendos. "That's right. He loves us anyway. He comes to that place in your heart that you don't want anyone to

---

2. Woman at the well sermon ideas are from Father John Ferone's sermon April 2008 on this Scripture reading.

see, and if you're willing to turn it over to Him, Jesus will turn that place into love."

I'm shaking now, and I can't control the tears trickling down my face. I fight to swallow the sob fighting to escape. I brush the wetness from my cheeks.

Dad discreetly lays his palm on my thigh. "You okay?" he whispers.

I nod and push back my tears. I need to regain my composure and save these emotions for later, when I can sort them out, when I'm alone. But I continue to weep on the inside. Jesus knows what I've done, and He loves me anyway.

Mom puts her arm around me and kisses me on the cheek like I'm a six-year-old. I know she's trying to be nurturing, but I feel foolish and obvious. I shrug off her arm.

"I'm okay," I whisper.

I've really known all along. Jesus knows Noah and I had sex. He knows everything. But I've been too fearful to admit it, because then I would have to face the next part. What does Jesus think of me now? But, He loves me. Still. So what next?

CHAPTER TWENTY-FIVE

As soon as we're in the car, Mom starts in on me. "Lindsey, sweetie, what happened in there? Is everything okay? Is there something you need to talk about?"

Where to start? Of course everything's not okay! Duh! And I do need to talk about it, but not with my parents. I love them and all, but they're not the ones to chat with about this one. Who can I talk to? Emma might understand, but she'll probably laugh at me. I don't want her to feel like I'm preaching chastity to her. She was freaked about possibly being pregnant, but she didn't seem worried about having sex. The gears in my head turn and churn. We're at a red light and Dad looks back. "Lindsey?"

I need to answer.

"I'm fine, really. It's just Emma. She has some stuff going on right now that's kind of private, but I just thought about her when I heard that sermon, and I'm so whipped and I'm PMSing. I think my emotions are just whacked."

"I've been praying for Emma," Mom says.

She seems to have fallen for it. I hate to lie to my parents. It makes me feel feverish, but I was thinking of Emma just then, and I am PMSing, and my emotions are absolutely whacked, so it's not a complete lie. Who am I kidding? It will have to do until I can get a handle on all of this. *Sorry, God. Again!*

"I won't pry into her affairs, but if she needs someone to talk to, let her know I'd be her substitute Mom."

This time my words are genuine. "Mom?"

"Um-humm," she says, digging in her purse.

"You're the best."

She reaches back and squeezes my hand. In her grip I feel love. Pastor John's words ring in my ears. "Jesus will turn that place into love." Jesus is here with me now, showing me it's okay. He's going to help me through this. I could talk to Mom and Dad about it, and it might be okay. I don't think I will, but I could.

"What am I? Chopped liver?" Dad laughs, breaking the weightiness of the moment.

"I love you too, Dad." I laugh.

When we get home, I snatch a Diet Coke from the fridge and a pack of frosted cherry Pop-Tarts from the pantry and head to my room. I grab my iPod, go to Artists, and select Todd Agnew. I slip my earbuds in, turn the volume down low, and flop onto my bed.

Okay, God, I pray. *I need You. I need You like I've never needed You before. I love Noah, and I love You. I know there would be no Noah without You. I truly believe You brought Noah into my life.* I take a deep breath.

I also know now You did not intend for us to sleep together. That is not Your plan. Not yet.

"I cannot believe I'm this dirty. I'm ashamed to even ask to be clean. I can't think of anyone less worthy. I have nothing to offer or to bring."[3] Todd Agnew's husky voice etches my own thoughts on my brain. A film of tears veils my eyes.

---

3. "Wait for Your Rain" Written by Todd Agnew © 2003 Koala Music (ASCAP) All Rights Reserved. Used by Permission.

So what now, God?

You have to tell Noah. You have to lay it out completely and not get distracted, no matter what he says or does, a Voice whispers into my heart.

Will I lose him?

You have to tell him and go from there. Trust Me.

I want God to say everything will be all right. Noah loves me, right? He wants to marry me. Doesn't that mean he'd do anything for me? I strain my ears and my heart listening for more direction, but all I hear is Todd Agnew. I wiggle my earbuds and wait for more from God.

Trust Me.

I want more. I want a guarantee! God isn't giving me any guarantee on my hockey girlfriend status. Am I willing to risk Noah to please God? I know in my soul I don't have a choice.

I'm sorry, Jesus. I'm so sorry. I get it. What I did was wrong because it defiled You. I gave away a gift that You gave me. Sleeping with Noah wasn't wrong because society thinks it was slutty. It wasn't wrong because I could have gotten pregnant or an STD, although either of those would be hideous. It was wrong because I threw away Your gift, because I went against Your Word." Tears pour out of me, washing my face as the confession washes my soul.

Thank You, I whisper. *Thank You for loving me, for forgiving me. Please give me the strength to do What I need to do next. I'm going to need You.* I exhale, and my shoulders let out the guilt they've been trying to balance for weeks.

CHAPTER TWENTY-SIX

My legs feel like Jell-O. My hair is stringy and sweaty and matted to my head. Todd worked our tails off at practice today, and I'm starving.

Mom sets dinner for two and pours Diet Coke in fancy wine glasses with lemon wedges on their rims. I plunge into my chair. "Just two?" I ask.

I stayed to myself most of yesterday. I needed time to think and pray about what to do next. Mom and Dad didn't seem to notice. They went on a walk and chopped and simmered the ingredients for Wiener schnitzel, laughing and talking in low voices while they made an authentic German family dinner. They really do seem to still love each other, even though they've been married for a million years and Dad travels all the time. I hope I have a marriage like that some day.

My brain flips to a movie of Noah and me in our twenties, riding bikes down a wooded lane, laughing on a picturesque fall day, and then to another scene of us clinking coffee mugs in a cozy breakfast nook with a newspaper spread out on a wooden table. I try to shake these reveries from my head. These are the images I can't allow myself to delve into.

"Dad had a day trip to Chicago. He'll be home tonight, but not until late." Mom places forks and knives by our plates. They clunk lightly on the farmer's table.

"Kristine's eating at Wes's house."

I nod. I've never eaten dinner at Noah's. How long after you've been sleeping with someone does that invite get extended? I slap myself inside my brain for my sarcasm.

"Lindsey, do you want to say the blessing, or should I?"

"You can, Mom." I put my napkin on my lap. The savory leftover Wiener schnitzel Mom heated up smells delicious. My growling stomach sounds louder than my hairdryer at full blast.

"Dear Lord, thank You for this time Lindsey and I have together. Please bring Dad home safely. Please be with Kristine." Mom's voice chokes. I keep my eyes closed, not wanting to embarrass her by seeing her cry. I hear her softly exhale.

"And please be with Lindsey's stomach. Apparently she's hungry." We both laugh, breaking the nervous mood constantly surrounding Kristine.

"So, what's the most important thing that happened to you today?" Mom quizzes, using knife and fork to cut the meat.

"Most important?" I'm stumped. The rich gravy trickles down my throat. "I don't know." Then it hits me. The most important thing that *could* happen to me today is to resolve this sex situation with Noah. I take a sip of my Diet Coke. The bubbles jump up and down on my tongue, urging me to spit out the words.

"Mom?" I ask.

She looks up from her plate.

"Well, you see, it's like this." I can't stop now, not even for air. "Noah and I disagree about something, and we agree about almost everything, and he's wonderful and kind and funny and treats me like a princess, but there's this one thing, you see? And, I just don't know what to do about it." I inhale and take another sip of soda.

"Well, I guess it depends on what you're disagreeing about." Mom leans back in her chair.

I nod. *Please don't ask, Mom. Please don't ask, Mom.* I silently plead.

"If it's something little, I've learned to let it go. If Noah is as wonderful as he seems, then you have to overlook the little stuff. That's how a relationship works. I certainly excuse a lot of Dad's quirks, and thankfully, he ignores mine."

I nod and chew and nod and chew.

"But, I'm guessing it's not something little?"

I shake my head. I can't speak. Anything I say at this point will be wrong. Mom hasn't asked, and I'm not ready to tell.

"Well, if it's something big, you need to talk to him about it." Mom's eyebrows do that crazy crooked thing they do when she's thinking really hard or is super worried. "Lindsey, can you tell me what it is?"

"Never mind," I mumble with my mouth full of food. It would be better to not hear the end of her advice than to divulge my secret.

Mom lets out a long sigh. "I wouldn't tell Noah that you're right and he's wrong. I'd just tell him this is something important to you and how you feel about it." Mom takes a bite of green beans. "Noah should respect your opinion and at least be open to discuss things. If not, I'm afraid he's not the young man you think he is."

Her words weave through my head like the stitches on my jeans, all precisely spaced and in a perfectly straight row.

"Thanks, Mom." I swallow. "That's what I thought, but it's weird . . . it helped to talk about it." I smile weakly. I never thought I'd consult my mom on sex.

"I'm glad." She cuts another bite of schnitzel. "I just wish I knew what we just talked about." Mom's laughter fills the room.

I spit out a mouth of Diet Coke and spray the table, sending us both into fits of giggles.

/ / /

While Mom clears the dishes, I pull out my phone—while I still have the courage.

"Mom," I shout toward the kitchen. "Is it all right if I go over and talk to him?"

"I thought that was the whole point." Mom laughs.

Noah answers on the first ring. "Hey."

"Hey." I feel like Queen Esther afraid to tell the king how she's going to be exiled by his right-hand man, Haman.

Dear God, I need You. Please give me the strength You gave Esther. I know this isn't nearly as important. I'm not saving the Jewish nation, but I do want to save myself.

That's plenty important, I feel God respond.

"Linds? You there?" Noah's thick voice probes.

I know I need to do this. I feel God's strength pulse through my veins. "Yeah, sorry about that, anyway, I was wondering if I could come over? I need to see you."

"I need to see you, too. I haven't been able to kiss those sweet lips of yours in forever."

"Hmmm." I feel his warm lips on mine. *Not now, girl,* I tell myself. "Kissing's nice, but I kind of want to talk, too."

"Talking's okay." I can hear Noah's smile. "Sure, come on over. We're just finishing up dinner."

"Us, too. Give me a few minutes to help Mom clean up, and I'll walk over."

"Why don't I start walking too, so I can meet you partway

and keep you safe in that wild neighborhood of ours?"

"Thanks. See you in about ten minutes?"

"Can't wait. Plus I can kiss you on the street before we even get back to my house. That way I get my kissing in."

"Devilish, aren't you?" I laugh.

"Somewhat." He snickers.

I snap my phone closed and wander back into the kitchen. I plop the rest of the green beans in a plastic tub and seal the lid. "He's home, Mom. So, I guess I'm goin' over."

Mom places her hand on my shoulder. "Lindsey, honey, you're doing the right thing." She takes the green beans from me and pops them in the fridge. "I'll be in the family room preparing for some of my sessions for tomorrow if you want to chat when you get home."

"Thanks, Mom." I hug her. She hugs back. Mom's always been a good hugger. I wash out our glasses and bound upstairs. I forgot I was so disgusting. At a minimum I need a one-minute shower to wash off the grime.

CHAPTER TWENTY-SEVEN

I see his silhouette before I hear his footsteps. Even though he's just a shadow, my mind fills in all the details from the rough edges on his fingernails to the way his left eyebrow is slightly higher than his right.

"I was beginning to worry about you." Noah's voice breaks the silence of suburban twilight.

"Sorry. I forgot I was completely disgusting and had to rinse off."

"You didn't have to primp for me." We're close enough now that he reaches out and grabs my hand. Under the streetlight he pulls me close and kisses me, like in the movies. I memorize the moment, knowing it might be our last embrace. I taste his mintyness and measure the pressure of his hands squeezing mine.

"Hi," he whispers.

"Hi." I bite my lower lip.

We start walking in the direction of his house, our hands still interlocked.

"So, what's up?" Noah asks.

"A lot, actually." I suck my lips in, smear my lip gloss evenly, and stop. "Remember that day in the cafeteria when I started babbling about chastity rings and all that?"

"Yeah."

"Well, I was so blown away, so completely overwhelmed when you told me you wanted to marry me. I mean, I love you so much, Noah, and I never knew I could feel this way about anybody, but I got so carried away that I never finished."

His deep green eyes search my face for a clue to where this is going. "I love you too. That's the whole point, Linds."

"Right, well, that's part of the point." The words tumble from my mouth. I have to keep going so I don't lose my train of thought like last time. "The other part is, well, I love God, too, and He doesn't want us to be sleeping together . . . not yet. Not until we're married."

Noah smiles. "We talked about this, Linds. I'm going to marry you. It's not like I'm with you for the sex. I'm with you because I love you."

I smile and look down, because if what he says is true, then everything is going to be okay. *Dear God, I want this all to be true, but I know it's in Your hands now.*

So keep going.

A car drives past. I can't breathe. I fear the driver can hear our conversation, can know what I've done. Its headlights illuminate Noah's face like the flash of a camera. He is so gorgeous, but I can't get swept away again. So, I take God's advice. I keep going.

I sigh. "See, if it's truly not about the sex, then we don't need it, right? God doesn't want us to be that intense yet. I think it's like when I was little and my parents wouldn't let me watch PG movies until I was eleven, and I couldn't understand because I felt like all my friends and everyone else in the world was watching them." I cock my head. I don't know if any of this is making sense to Noah, but it's all becoming so clear to me. With each word it becomes clearer and clearer.

"But then, when I saw that movie *Narnia,* I bawled when

all those evil creatures tied up Aslan, you know, the lion, and killed him. I had nightmares about those witches and ogres for weeks. Then, I got it. I could barely handle that PG movie at eleven, let alone when I was younger. I think sex is like that." I nod at my own explanation. "I know that it seems like everyone else is doing it. And I couldn't understand why it's not okay for us, since I know we have so much more, but it's just not. Not now." I shuffle my shoe on the ground. "What is it the Bible says in First Corinthians 13? 'Now we see in a mirror, dimly, but then face to face'?[4] We're not mature enough yet." I shift feet.

Noah coughs.

Aaaargh! What is *he* thinking? He hasn't said anything. I don't want Noah to think I'm saying he's immature. "I mean you're amazingly mature and smart and sensitive, but even though our bodies might be ready for sex — it felt great and everything — I don't think God made our emotions ready for sex until we're married." I take a deep gulp of air and look into Noah's beautiful eyes, finally certain of where I stand — even if I don't have a clue where Noah and I stand. "At least I know *my* emotions aren't ready."

"I love you, Lindsey." It's dark, and I can't read the expression on his face. He pulls me to his strong form and holds me.

"I love you too, but I love God even more." There, I've said it. I've said it all.

I don't know what will happen next. I want Noah to still be my boyfriend but in a sexually pure kind of way. He might not be able to have that kind of relationship. Or, he might not want one. Or, he might just be done, be saying good-bye. But, no matter what the outcome, I feel better than I have in weeks — better than when Noah told me he loved me on Valentine's, better than when

---

4. Verse 12, NKJV.

he said he wanted to marry me. All that time I was still carrying around the guilt and uncertainty about what we had done. Now, my heart is clean again. At least it's pure. And I trust with all my soul that *God* will be here to hold me tomorrow, even if Noah can't.

ABOUT THE AUTHOR

I believe in God. I believe in true love. I believe in fairies. I believe if I bang hard enough on the back of my wardrobe I'll get to Narnia someday. I believe eating chocolate is good for you. I believe part of my soul lives in France, part at the beach, and the other part here in Oxford, Ohio, because when I go to those places I feel at home, as if I've always belonged. I believe heaven will feel much the same. I believe God created me to be the wife of my husband, the mother of my four children, and to write the stories He wanted to tell. Visit Laura L. Smith's website at www.lauralsmith.net.

If you liked *Hot*, then you'll love *Skinny*!

Skinny
Laura L. Smith
978-1-60006-356-5

She was starving to fit in.

Teen Melissa Rollins is determined to have the perfect body, even if it makes her throw up. Whether you're a young woman, a mom, or a youth pastor, you'll appreciate the truth and compassion in Melissa's struggle with anorexia. Will she hear God's voice before it's too late?

Check out the online discussion guide for *Skinny* at www.navpress.com.

Coming September 2010: *Angry* "She was screaming to be heard."

To see other teen fiction novels from the TH1NK line of NavPress, go to TH1NKbooks.com. To order copies, call NavPress at 1-800-366-7788 or log on to www.navpress.com.

NAVPRESS   **TH1NK**

NavPress - A Ministry of The Navigators

*Wherever you are in your spiritual journey,
NavPress will help you grow.*

The NavPress mission is to advance the calling of The Navigators by publishing life-transforming products that are biblically rooted, culturally relevant, and highly practical.

www.navpress.com   1-800-366-7788

NAVPRESS

GLEN EYRIE

Glen Eyrie Spiritual Retreats

Glen Eyrie offers an ongoing lineup of retreats for Men, Women, Couples, and Ministry Leaders. Our desire is for these retreats to strengthen the foundations of your faith and to cause you to go deeper in your relationship with God!

Please visit our website for information on different spiritual retreats you can attend, dates, costs, and availability.

www.gleneyrie.org/retreats

GLEN EYRIE
Christian Camps and Conferences